REAL? OR IMAGINED?

In all the places Will had been in his life, and all the years he'd spent in Yellowstone, he had never seen anything as beautiful as the Grand Geyser. He'd watched it erupt countless times, and it was never the same twice. Old Faithful impressed the tourists. Giant and Giantess were rare amazements. Sawmill's exuberance was charming. But nothing could ever be like the Grand.

So he could be forgiven for not noticing exactly when it was that he saw what he saw.

He'd all but forgotten it by the time it was over, by the time the pool emptied after five wonderful bursts. But five-year-old Chuck was squirming now, and pulled off Will's hat in a bid to reclaim his attention. "Let me down!"

Will wasn't quite sure what made him look back over through the clearing steam again as he rescued his hat and lifted the boy down, but when he did, he almost dropped him.

There was something there. At first he thought it was just a pile of - something - down the slope a bit, almost out of sight. But then he heard the moan.

Books by M.M. Justus

Much Ado in Montana

Cross-Country: Adventures Alone Across America and Back

Tales of the Unearthly Northwest

Sojourn

Time in Yellowstone

Repeating History
True Gold
"Homesick"

Finding Home

HOMESICK

A TIME IN YELLOWSTONE STORY

M.M. JUSTUS

Carbon
River
Press

Homesick

HOMESICK

I

Ranger Will McManis didn't know what to be, whether happy or sad or anything in between, as he clumped along the deserted trail in Yellowstone National Park's Upper Geyser Basin making his rounds. It would have been a crowded sunny August afternoon in a normal year. But 1945 wasn't a normal year by any stretch of the imagination. Not 1945 or the three years before it.

World War II had officially ended four days ago with the capitulation of the Japanese. Celebrations had broken out all over the country, or so they'd heard on the radio. The war was over, and now life could get back to normal. It would take a while, though. Visiting national parks was still a long way down on anyone's list of priorities, even if gasoline wasn't still being rationed so they could get here.

But Will's mother was gone, and Will's life would never get back to normal. She'd passed away on V-J day as if she'd been waiting for the war to end, even though she had no stake in the business herself. Well, that wasn't true. They'd all had a stake in it, as patriotic Americans in general, and in the family members who were even now waiting their turn on the troopships headed for home in specific. Will's family had been one of the lucky ones. Several of his younger relatives had been of the right age to enlist, and they'd fought and survived. As was not the case for so many other families, everyone they loved was coming home intact and alive.

But Will's mother would not be waiting for them. Her only grandson had already done his stint in the first world war. James was safely in Denver being the family anomaly. He'd been an anomaly from the day Will and Karin had met him. He's a successful businessman, Will reminded himself. Successful and happy, or he had been until Catherine died five years ago. No one could blame him for closing himself away after his wife died in childbirth, least of all his adoptive parents.

It had been too much like Karin's second miscarriage, only worse. Will and James had almost lost her right here in the winterkeeper's quarters at the Old Faithful Inn thirty-odd years ago. But by the grace of God she'd lived in spite of the winter isolation of the Upper Geyser Basin in the old days.

He hadn't realized how much the awful experience had affected then fifteen-year-old James, but the boy, odd at the best of times, had never been the same. Will hadn't, either. But her near-death hadn't changed Will completely the way it had James. James's wife's death had been too much like what had almost happened to James's beloved mother, only worse. James had even shut himself away from the only light to come from the tragedy.

That light was bouncing down the trail towards Will this very moment, even as Will was thinking about how much James had missed by cutting himself off from his only child up until now. James's five-year-old son, Charles Patrick McManis, familiarly called Chuck, was named after his paternal great-grandfather. Chuck was an unmitigated joy, if one of the most mischievous children Will had ever had the pleasure to meet.

Will shook himself, trying to throw his morbid mood off like his father's heavy old coat, and held out his arms as Chuck barreled into him.

"Granddad! Granddad!"

Will swung his grandson's little body up onto his shoulders with a grunt. "You're getting heavy, boy. What's Grandmother been feeding you this morning, rocks?"

The child laughed, the sound bright as a bell. However, welcome as the boy's presence was, and Will realized that he did welcome him in spite of the need he'd thought he'd had to be alone this morning, Chuck shouldn't be out here by himself. Will tilted his head around to eye Chuck's deceptively innocent-looking face. "Where is your grandmother? Does she know you're out here?"

Will already knew the answer to that one. No, she didn't, because she'd have never allowed the boy out here alone. If they'd developed one iron-clad rule since Chuck learned to walk, it was "Never, ever, ever, go anywhere by yourself." It was simply too dangerous in this place, in too many ways. The open space in front of their quarters was as far as the boy was allowed to go alone, and even then Karin kept a sharp eye on him.

Chuck scowled. "She said wait a minute and I'll take you. She said it *five times*."

Will seriously doubted that. He should have taken Chuck with him this morning. He almost always did. With the park all but closed down for the duration of the war, he was mostly a glorified watchman. Only a couple of dozen rangers were scattered across the park after the rest of them had either enlisted, been drafted, or were simply let go as a low priority during wartime. The few left behind were only here because they'd refused to leave.

But he'd been low. A foolish excuse. Will was smiling now in spite of himself and he knew it. He schooled his features into sternness and knew he succeeded when Chuck's own face fell. "Granddad."

"Do you know what we need to do?"

Chuck shook his blond head so hard Will could feel the breeze.

"I think you do." Will headed back down the trail towards their quarters in the little cluster of cabins used by the permanent rangers. Theirs was only one of three occupied these last three years. "I think we need to go find Grandmother so you can apologize to her for running off. I'm sure she's very worried about you."

And indeed, he could see the relief in Karin's eyes after they rounded the last corner and found her, having followed the sound of her voice calling Chuck's name.

"Oh, *skatten min*, you scared me," she told Chuck, the endearment a relic of her Norwegian-American childhood.

Will gave the boy a firm nod and swung him down. Chuck ran to her, wrapping his little arms around her thighs. "I'm sorry, Grandmother."

"You won't do it again, will you?"

Karin glanced over the boy's head at Will, her expression wry, even as Chuck said, "I won't," as solemnly as he was capable of, given that his face was buried in the apron she wore over her jeans. She'd acquired a taste for wearing men's clothing during the Klondike gold rush, and indulged in it on their isolated duty here. He raised his head. "You won't say 'in a minute' anymore?"

Both adults laughed in spite of themselves. Karin crouched down to his level, hugged him, then put a finger under his chin, lifting his gaze to meet her own. "*Skatten min*, sometimes we don't always get what we want when we want it. Sometimes you have to wait."

Chuck started to stamp his foot, then caught Will's eye. Will shook his head.

It was hard to deny the boy anything, especially when they knew they were counting days till his father would finally be taking him home to Denver to start school. They'd had Chuck since he was a newborn, ever since a grief-stricken James had asked them to take him in, "just for a while." Neither Will nor Karin could have said no to him then, for the baby's sake as much as for their son's, but a month had stretched into two, into six, into a year, and here they all still were, five years later.

James had never visited as much as he could, but it was hard to condemn him for it given his inexplicable dislike of the park. Not completely unaccountable, Will supposed, no matter how irrational. James had loved Yellowstone as much as the rest of them before Karin's miscarriage. But Karin in particular hadn't been able to condemn him for it. She and young Jem, as he'd been known then, had formed an instant bond the moment they met, upon their return from the Klondike. James had been five years old, too, in the company of Will's own parents. They'd never been able to explain the child's presence, at least not to Will's satisfaction, the only story they'd told them one he'd never been able to believe.

But Karin had fallen in love that day, for the second time in mere months. The first, Will thought with satisfaction even after all these years, had been with him. And that, he'd discovered soon after, was that. Will found himself taken in by the darkhaired young scoundrel, and party to Karin's adoption of him as their own almost before he knew what happened.

And now here was another five year old miscreant who had them wrapped around his little fingers. At least Will's father had never claimed the namesake he'd predicted Catherine would bear was a time traveler.

* * *

"- I really can't keep an eye on him this morning," Karin was saying after she rose back to her feet. "Can't you take him with you?"

"Reward him for running off?" Will asked, raising an eyebrow at her. And it was a reward. They both knew there was nothing little Chuck liked better than going with his grandfather on his rounds.

"Please, Granddad? Please?"

The boy would simply try to pester Karin into bringing him out. And while she was perfectly capable of withstanding him, it would make them both unhappy. Besides, what had Will been doing when the boy'd come chasing after him? Moping, that was what. Which was no use whatsoever, to him or anyone else, as his mother would have said. Will sighed and capitulated. "I guess."

"Yay!" Chuck bounced on his heels.

"But only if you promise, next time, when you're supposed to stay home with Grandmother, you stay with Grandmother."

"I promise." And he meant it, as much as a child his age could. They were working on it. All three of them. Will wondered, not for the first time, if James had any idea what he was going to be getting himself into when he came to pick the boy up next week.

"Come in and have something to eat first, before you go back out."

"Grandmother's making lefse," Chuck said confidingly.

"Is she?" Will smiled at his wife. "What were you going to do with them if we didn't show up? Eat them all up on your own?"

"I was going to come get you myself." She reached down and tweaked Chuck's ear. He jumped back and grinned up at her. "And bring Chuck with me. If he'd just waited one minute longer."

But the boy's attention was now elsewhere, on one of the ubiquitous crickets bounding along the ground this time of year. One of his favorite pastimes this summer was to see how close he could creep up on one before it leaped.

"Look, Granddad!" he shouted as the inch-long bug sprang away on its long legs. He held out his hands about a foot apart. "I got this close!"

"I see, Chuck," Will said. "Come on in."

Their quarters were dim and cool after the bright sunshine outside, but the kitchen smelled of blackberry jam, and, once Karin heated the cast-iron skillet and poured the first round of lefse batter, of warm potato pancake.

The first one went to Chuck, who promptly dripped blackberry jam down his front. It didn't decrease his enjoyment of the treat one bit, however, nor Will's as he watched his grandson devour it.

He bit into the second one himself, and, reminded, was glad he was where he was and not in the bitter Yukon winter where he'd eaten his first one. "Somehow these just don't taste the same when I'm not freezing my tuckus off," he told Karin, not for the first time.

"I certainly hope not," was her standard response, then "Chuck, mind your fingers," as the boy tried to grab his second lefse while it was still too hot to handle.

"What are your plans for the day?" Will asked her.

She looked down at Chuck, who was now preoccupied with a spider crawling up the kitchen wall next to his chair, and grimaced but didn't object just then. It wasn't, Will saw gratefully, following her gaze, a recluse this time, but just a plain house spider. Ridding their quarters of spiders was an ongoing battle. "I need to go shopping. For his S-C-H-O-O-L clothes."

Will saw the boy stiffen at the spelled word which was, at his age, more wishful thinking on Karin's part than anything else, but only for a second. The spider was just too much of a temptation for him, as was, so far as Will could tell, every other living thing he ran across. And he ran across a great many of them here. Will himself was a bit more particular about his faunal interests, but he had been the one to encourage the boy in his, so he couldn't complain.

"James will do that, I'm sure." He had the money to do so, too. One of their biggest bones of contention over the last five years was their son's insistence on giving them money for the boy's "upkeep," as he called it. They took it - a ranger's salary was not anywhere near as large as that of a successful accountant - but it stuck in Will's craw. It did not in Karin's.

"James has no idea what Chuck needs," Karin said tartly. "The least we can do is get him started. Besides," she hesitated. "He asked me to. And sent a check to pay for it. I thought I'd go to Bozeman."

"All the way to Bozeman? Can't you get what you need in West?" The small tourist town of West Yellowstone was less than an hour's drive away. Bozeman, college town and their nearest city of any size, was a good two hours or more.

"You know full well they don't have what he needs in West."

"I guess. But isn't it too late to go that far?" He didn't want her driving back after dark. God knew what she'd run into. His vision ran to elk, bear, maybe even a buffalo. And a buffalo would total their old truck.

"It's only nine now, and it still doesn't get dark until eight these days." She read his mind, as she was wont to do, with the ease of long familiarity and knowledge of what he worried most about. "I'll be back before then. Can you fend for yourselves in the meantime? There's cold cuts in the refrigerator, and bread in the breadbox."

"Is there enough gas in the truck? Are there any ration coupons left?" They received a slightly higher gas ration because of where they were and what they were doing, but not that much more.

"I think so. There's still one unused sticker on the coupon, too."

Reluctantly, Will capitulated again. "We can fend for ourselves."

"What's fend?" The spider was gone, and Chuck was back at the table, grabbing for another potato pancake.

"Fend means take care of yourselves while I go to Bozeman today. Did you touch that spider, young man?" Karin demanded, batting his hands away from the plate.

"No. Whatcha gonna do?"

"I am going shopping."

Will knew as well as Karin did what Chuck thought of shopping. He grinned as the boy responded predictably. "Ick."

"Are you sure you didn't touch it? Maybe you'd better go wash your hands, anyway."

Will and Chuck had both washed their hands after they'd first walked in the door. Chuck pouted. "I didn't!"

Will put in, "He didn't, Karin. I watched."

"All right." After Chuck had grabbed his lefse she got up to clear the table, ruffling his hair in the process. It was an unruly mop. Will supposed she'd cut it before James arrived, too. Poor kid. Chuck had no idea how his life was going to change in a few days, and no amount of explanation was going to prepare him.

II

The whole place, not just their quarters, always seemed so quiet and empty when Karin was away. Oh, they weren't the only people here. Two other rangers shared Will's duties in the Upper Geyser Basin. The bare minimum of concessions staff operating the lone store sold the few goods available to the occasional local who had the gas to get this far, too, and also kept an eye on the closed-up lodge and Inn. But even with the boy trotting alongside him on the edge of the road, chattering at him, asking question after question and telling him about everything he saw, Will didn't want to think about how quiet things would get after Chuck left for Denver.

Yes, the child had to go to school, and no, it wasn't practical to drive him to West every day. Since the war started and the park staff went down to a skeleton crew, the school for employees' children at Mammoth Hot Springs, like everything else, shut down for the duration. And Chuck needed to go to school. Karin had taught him as much as he'd sit still for. The boy could count and recite his ABCs, and even read a little, and he probably knew as much about plants and animals as most children twice his age, although that had been Will's contribution in addition to Karin's. But he needed to go to school. Will just wished he didn't have to go all the way to Denver to do it.

If Will had one regret in life, it was that he and Karin had been unable to have children of their own. James had been adopted, and they'd come close a couple of times only for Karin to miscarry, but while he wouldn't have traded his wife for one who could give him a family for all the world, and he knew she felt the same about him, it was still - well, it was a regret. One he knew she carried as well.

He had to get out of this mood, Will thought as Chuck towed him by the hand across the bridge over the Firehole River near the boarded-up lodge. He needed to snap out of it, not that his surroundings were helping. The lodge looked forlorn, even abandoned, but then so did most of the buildings in the park. They had since December four years ago, when the Japs bombed Pearl Harbor and the world changed, but their state had never bothered him before. Soon those buildings would be back open and filled with people, now that the war was over. Next summer, he bet. As soon as the gas rationing let up.

"Look, Granddad!" The boy was peering between the railings of the bridge, staring down at the water in utter fascination, as usual. No matter how many times he spotted a critter, it was always new to him. Will tightened his grip on the little fist. The last thing either of them needed was for Chuck to take a header into the river. "Look! Fish!"

"I see. Do you know what kind they are?"

"Trout!"

"That's right. Cutthroat trout."

The boy gazed up at him hopefully. "Can we go fishing?"

"Maybe later. We need to make our rounds first. Come on."

Chuck didn't cast a backwards glance, but went on willingly. The child was spoiled for things to fascinate him here. Will sometimes wondered if he missed other children, but perhaps he didn't know the difference.

Will ambled down the trail, moderating his pace to Chuck's shorter steps, stopping frequently to examine one thing or another. His 'rounds', as he thought of them, through the geyser basin weren't really necessary, not like the ones he and the other rangers made through the government buildings, looking for critter break-ins and weather damage and making repairs. But he kept some records, made some notes, to keep up as much as he could so that there wouldn't be complete gap in the scientific record once the rest of the naturalists returned. And he kept a record of the rare visitors who managed to find the gasoline to make the trip. Mostly the few locals who had B ration stickers for one reason or another. The park wasn't officially closed, even if everything was shut down.

Chuck began to lag. His little legs were more accustomed to long tramps than most children's his age, Will suspected, but he usually ended up carrying the boy at least part of the way. "Ready for a ride, cowboy?" Will grasped Chuck around his waist and swung him up to his shoulders.

Chuck laughed and pointed. "I can see better than you!"

Sure enough, one of the marmots that made its home in the geyser basin was perched on a rock a few yards away. It watched them curiously. The critter was young, used to them, and to the peace and quiet of the war years. It was going to be in for a rude awakening once things got back to normal. Will stopped and they watched it for a bit, but when it simply sat there and watched them back, Will started forward again. They were almost upon it when it finally lumbered off, down the trail instead of away from it.

They came out of the lodgepole pine forest onto the open sinter crust of Geyser Hill. Another reason he'd picked the boy up. The trail was narrow here, and a step wrong could put even a child's foot right through to a boiling spring, with disastrous results. There'd been talk for a while about putting up boardwalks, and a few had been built by the CCC boys back in the thirties, along with a lot of other improvements, but they hadn't gotten any work done here.

Will stopped to see what, if anything, Giantess was doing today. Chuck leaned over in imitation, and Will pulled on his feet, regaining their equilibrium with the ease of long practice. Geysers weren't the boy's first love, the way they were Will's. Will suspected it was a matter of patience. Critters were here, there, and everywhere. Geysers made you wait for them, and waiting had never been one of the boy's talents.

Giantess's pool hadn't changed since the last time he'd checked. The water was at the same level, and the occasional bubble reached the surface and broke with a watery belch. Giantess didn't erupt to anyone's schedule, and so seldom that Will himself had only seen it erupt three times in all his years here.

Speaking of geysers, however, across the river Old Faithful gave a splash, then another, and rose into the air. But when a geyser erupts every hour or so, eventually it's no longer a novelty. Will picked his way carefully along the sinter trail and down the other side of Geyser Hill towards his favorite of the smaller geysers to see if Sawmill was erupting today.

Everything he'd thought about familiarity breeding indifference with regard to Old Faithful could be applied equally to Sawmill Geyser. In fact, when it was active its eruptions often lasted longer than the gaps in between them. But he wasn't quite sure why this little geyser never bored him. Karin sometimes said it was because it just looked like it was having such a good time, flinging water with such abandon, chugging along in its characteristic way that made the very ground vibrate nearby.

But then Karin tended to talk about the geysers as if they were human, or at least sentient. As did a great many of the visitors to the park. What amused Will most, and always had, was the way eruptions of Old Faithful sometime elicited applause. Take a bow, Sawmill, he thought, as he and the boy watched the little geyser churn. Your audience will be back soon.

* * *

They cut back across the second bridge to the road, and Will let Chuck down onto his own feet. Will looked for signs of a recent eruption at Castle Geyser, and then eyed Chuck. His ride seemed to have rested him, and Will was curious.

"Let's go a bit further."

"Okay." The boy trotted along, stopping to poke and peer and play his cricket game. Will kept an eye on him, and on the springs and various runoff channels along the way, noting changes - seldom - and nothing new - frequent - in the water levels and behavior.

By the time they got to Grotto Geyser, which was churning away, generating clouds of steam, Chuck was beginning to flag again, and, besides, Will knew, they'd both be getting hungry soon.

"Here. Hold my notebook." He handed over the worn, palm-sized spiral-bound notebook and his pencil, then put the boy up on his shoulders again, and they turned back, taking the path this time instead of retracing their steps along the road. They crossed the river one more time, and Will strode along, his hands on Chuck's ankles. He could feel his notebook sitting on top of his head in Chuck's grasp, and, after a moment the notebook started thumping in rhythm with his steps. "Hey. Quit that."

Chuck laughed, and kept thumping.

Will tugged on his ankle. "I mean it."

"It's a drum!"

"No, my head is not a drum. Do you want down?" Will reached up to the boy's waist.

"No!" But he stopped thumping. For now, anyway.

They passed Giant Geyser, with its broken tree trunk shaped cone and wisps of steam. Will didn't stop, although he wanted to. He always wanted to. He'd only seen Giant erupt once in all his years here, and it had been a sight to behold. But he kept going, only occasionally stopping to ask Chuck for his notebook and to tell the boy to hold on tight while Will made his notes, then handing them back and moving on.

Chuck was beginning to squirm by the time they came within sight of the Grand, and reluctantly Will let him down, keeping a firm grip on the boy's hand and rolling his shoulders to ease the strain. He wondered how much longer he'd be able to carry the child around like that. Not that it mattered. He suspected that once James got the boy back to Denver, it would be a very long time before he brought Chuck here again. Yellowstone hadn't been James's favorite place since he was fifteen, to put it mildly, even if Denver wasn't so far away. And here he thought he'd banished all his morbid, sad thoughts, for the day, at least.

"Look, Granddad!" Chuck tugged on his hand, his timing, as ever, better than a five-year-old's had a right to be. "Look at the water!"

Will looked. The Grand's pool *was* full. And the runoff channels were rippling with the overflow. He grinned. Well, if this wasn't an improvement to his day he didn't know what was. "Want to stay and watch?"

"Yeah!" Chuck bounced.

All right, so the boy liked geysers, too, not just the critters. As long as he didn't have to wait hours for them, which was reasonable. James had been almost preternaturally patient when he was that age, although, Will had to admit, only when it came to geysers.

They picked their way across the runoff rivulets to the other side so they wouldn't have to do it afterwards when the water would be deep enough to get their boots wet, and fetched up near a lone wind-warped lodgepole pine. The tree had grown just out of reach of the Grand's runoff channels for as long as Will could remember. He boosted Chuck up onto a notch formed by one of those odd branches. The child was going to be too big for that seat soon, but for now it was the perfect place to keep him safe during the eruption. Will kept a hand on his ankle, just in case, and made himself comfortable against the tree's trunk.

Will couldn't think of anywhere he'd rather be just now. He suspected his mother, whose favorite geyser this had been, would approve of them staying to watch it, too. He suspected she'd have preferred her funeral be here rather than in the chapel at Mammoth Hot Springs, but it wouldn't have been proper, which had always mattered more to her. Besides, it had been difficult enough for family to get that far, let alone all the way here. Things had been different when his father died. The war hadn't started yet in 1939, with the worst of the Great Depression in the rear-view mirror.

"Look, son." Will pointed. The little round mound of Turban Geyser, next to the Grand, was erupting to its usual magnificent height of three feet. They both watched it, and the Grand's pool. Turban was what was called an indicator. It was all kind of like a logic puzzle with the Grand. Everything has to be just so. The pool has to be overflowing, not just full. Turban has to start first. The level in the pool can't drop while Turban is playing- Will sighed. There went the Grand's pool, not down by much unless you knew what you were looking for, but enough. "Not this time."

"Next time?"

Will eyed him. "Do you really want to wait?"

"Can we?"

Well. That was a surprise. "Of course we can."

Turban was more regular than Old Faithful, and even more frequent, about every twenty minutes or so. The Grand was already overflowing again, a good sign that next time might be it.

Will tugged on Chuck's foot, gently, so the boy wouldn't lose his balance, and when Chuck gave him an indignant glance, he grinned back. "Don't fall."

"Oh, Granddad." Then he looked away. Will followed his gaze. Of course. A marmot. Another marmot, to go with the one they'd seen earlier. This one was large in comparison to the other critter. Will wondered how old it was, if it remembered crowds sharing its home. It sat on the hill behind the Grand, watching them with about as much curiosity as they watched him.

A raven joined the party a few minutes later, poking around in one of the runoff channels, then another flew in, and another, croaking at each other, sounding for all the world as if they were carrying on some sort of long, involved conversation. One flew up and perched on a branch of their pine less than six feet from Chuck, who reached out to it. The bird cocked an eye back at him and let out a croak, almost deafening at this close a range.

"What's he trying to tell you?" Will asked.

"He's waiting, too. He likes his water hot," said Chuck.

It was an interesting leap of logic, for lack of a better term. Will laughed. "Then he's in the right place, isn't he?"

The runoff began to ripple again. Turban began to bubble. Grand's pool began to boil. Chuck bounced on his branch. "Granddad!"

And a fountain of water burst into the sky.

III

In all the places Will had been in his life, and all the years he'd spent in Yellowstone, he had never seen anything as beautiful as the Grand Geyser. He'd watched it erupt countless times, and it was never the same twice. Old Faithful impressed the tourists. Giant and Giantess were rare amazements. Sawmill's exuberance was charming. But nothing could ever be like the Grand.

So he could be forgiven, Will supposed later, for not noticing exactly when it was that he saw what he saw.

His first glimpse of it was out of the corner of his eye. His attention was divided between the exuberant fountain of water and the boy bouncing on his branch, his little booted feet banging against both the tree and Will's shoulder in his excitement. Will merely glanced at it, then back to the main event.

When the eruption paused between bursts, he turned his head again, but couldn't see anything through the steam. He shrugged.

Then the water flung itself up again. And again. And again. There was a reason geysers were said to play, Will thought, and wished Karin was here to make him eat crow on the subject as she always did. The Grand was obviously having a terrific time, the concussion of two-hundred foot tall sprays of water shaking the ground, as if someone down deep was setting off a cannon. Or as if somehow a tidal wave could travel underground and burst upward. He would never, ever get tired of watching this. He knew he was grinning at it and couldn't stop. He never could.

He'd all but forgotten the odd thing he'd seen by the time it was over, by the time the pool emptied and the hiss of the runoff disappeared after five wonderful bursts. But Chuck was squirming now, and pulled off Will's hat in a bid to reclaim his attention. "Let me down!"

Will wasn't quite sure what made him look back over through the clearing steam one more time as he rescued his hat and lifted the boy down, but when he did, he almost dropped him.

There *was* something there. At first he thought it was just a pile of - something - over on the other side of the runoff channel, down the slope a bit, almost out of sight. But then he heard the moan.

* * *

Will hesitated. It almost sounded human, but that was impossible. He glanced down at Chuck, who was staring in the same direction he was. No, Chuck wasn't who the sound had come from, but he'd known that already. It wasn't - even though he wanted it to be - it wasn't trees creaking in the wind. There was no wind. The Grand's steam had gone almost straight up into the sky. And even if there had been, he knew the difference between a human voice and the rubbing of one tree branch against another.

Chuck tugged on his hand and pointed. "The lady's hurt." *Lady?* Chuck tugged on his hand again. "Come on!"

Almost blindly Will picked the boy up again before he could get himself in trouble, and picked his way across the now drying but still slippery sinter down the slope towards the - whatever it was. Once he got a few steps nearer it resolved into what looked like a pile of wet, dirty flowered fabric. Until Will leaned over more closely and saw the arm flung out in the opposite direction, and a spray of long, reddish-brown hair.

"Dear God," Will said, forgetting himself for the first time, and set the boy down. "Do not move," he told Chuck firmly. "Not an inch." He crouched down beside the woman, for that's what she was.

She was young, late teens or early twenties, and wearing a long skirted dress trailing over one ankle and hiked up on the other leg almost to her knee. A bonnet trailed down her back, and her muddy shoes - buttoned? - up over her ankles. Old-fashioned. Everything she wore looked so old-fashioned -

Chuck squatted beside him in spite of his edict and reached out. Will grabbed the boy's hand before he could touch her. "Wait. She might be hurt." It was obvious that she *was* hurt. But it was equally

24

obvious that she couldn't stay here. Helplessly, Will pulled his gaze from her, down across the river and up to the Inn and the other buildings. He couldn't send the boy for anyone. For one thing, he couldn't send a five-year-old that far by himself anywhere, let alone in a dangerous place like this. For another, even if he did send the boy, the other rangers could be anywhere. There was no one to fetch to help get her to safety, and the last thing she needed was to be slung over his shoulder in a fireman's carry, which was the only way he was going to be able to get her there by himself. He'd never been so unhappily conscious of how alone they were before.

Tentatively, he reached out to touch her, then pulled his hand back as she stirred. "Don't move, miss, er, ma'am. Are you hurt anywhere? Do you feel any pain?"

She moved, anyway. Or tried to. She made another sound, not quite a moan this time, but half-formed words. "Where? Wha-?" Her voice was so faint he could barely hear her.

"Where do you hurt?" He couldn't let her lie here like this. Delicately, he reached out to touch her back, to try to assess the damage, and his hand went right through the cotton of her dress, right through her skin and muscle and bone as if it wasn't even *there*. Will jerked back, rocked on his heels and overbalanced himself, landing on his backside on the hard rock.

"What the-?!" He righted himself and stared.

He probably would have sat there staring for who knew how long, if it hadn't been for Chuck grabbing onto him. "Granddad, whatcha gonna do?"

What *could* he do? What he wanted to do was grab the boy up and run as far and as fast as he could, back to the Inn, back to their quarters, back to - no, not back to, back *away*. Instead he took Chuck's hand and rose slowly to his feet, bringing the reluctant child with him. Reluctant? What an understatement. The boy resisted so hard he would have pulled Will back down with him if their relative strength had been equal.

"No, Granddad! She's hurt!"

"Come on, Chuck." Will picked the boy up. "We have to go now."

"No!" Chuck kicked and flailed and squirmed, and Will almost dropped him. Did drop him when the boy twisted as he tried to heft the child to get a better grip on him.

Chuck dodged when Will tried grab him again, and plunked himself back down beside the - ghost? Illusion? Whatever it was, he had to get Chuck away from it. Now.

Before Will could get hold of him, Chuck reached out to her- it. Will watched, feeling frozen, helpless. The boy touched its- her- hair. Petted it. The hair slipped through the child's fingers, like real hair. Will jerked himself out of his paralysis and tried to touch it himself. It was as if it wasn't there.

"She's hurt, Granddad." The trust in the child's voice, that he could fix anything, wrenched Will's heart. She was much more than hurt, he thought wildly. She wasn't there. Except that *Chuck* could touch her. Will couldn't, but Chuck could.

Will took a deep breath. "Can you feel her neck?"

Chuck's dirty little fingers pushed at the hair.

"Be careful. You don't want to hurt her any worse."

Will could see her neck now. It did not look damaged, but how could he tell from merely looking? At someone who did not exist? He steeled himself - dear God, it was harder than anything he'd ever done - and tried to touch her head. He felt something this time. Not solid, but something.

All right. "Can you run your hand along her back? Along the buttons?" Will didn't know much about women's clothing, other than the fact that his wife preferred men's trousers when she could get away with it, and that she'd been very, very glad when corsets went out of style decades ago. This woman's clothes looked even more old-fashioned than the dresses his mother had worn when he was a child. "Tell me if you feel anything-" how was he to describe what he was looking for to a five-year-old? "-anything strange," he finished lamely.

"No." Chuck's voice sounded far more sure than it should have. Will steeled himself again, and reached out to try one more time. And almost overbalanced himself again jerking back. He *had* felt something this time. Cool metal buttons, cloth - and the firmness of the body underneath them.

So she *was* real. And he'd been imagining things. Will let out a sigh that ruffled the woman's tangled hair. "Ma'am? Can you roll over?"

She made a sound again, half moan and half word. He thought he heard "-try" before she made an abortive attempt.

"Let me help you." He reached out, slid his arms under her - it was much easier than it should have been, but he firmly believed he'd been imagining things now - and tried to lift her. She moaned, but didn't budge. She wasn't that heavy. He couldn't imagine what -

"Granddad." Chuck tugged on his arm.

Will slid his arms out from under her and sat back on his heels. "Just a second, son."

"Granddad."

"What?"

"She's going away."

"*What*?!"

He stared at her. Reached out. She felt solid to him. Too solid, almost. But the boy reached out again, too, and his hand went right through - Will grabbed Chuck's arm and pulled him back. "Don't touch her. She's hurt." It wasn't completely a lie. If the woman was a ghost, she was dead, which was about as hurt as it was possible to be. "Come here."

Chuck came to him, far too easily. The boy was frightened now, as frightened as -. Will wrapped his arms around the child and tried to stand, but Chuck started fighting him again and it was go back down or lose his balance and fall again himself.

Will sat down hard on the sinter, feeling it reverberate under his hindquarters. Chuck quit kicking and flailing and settled down, almost too quietly.

"What are we gonna do, Granddad?"

What *could* they do? "I don't know, son." But Will was, at last, starting to put two and two together.

Time travel, huh, Dad? He hadn't really believed what his father had told him, less than a year before the old man died, and then only, as Charley McManis had said, because Will needed to know, to perpetuate the cycle. The Möbius strip, his father had called it, a term Will barely remembered from his college days and which made no sense at all in this context.

In 1937 his father had dragged Will to a lawyer's office in Denver, of all places, not Bozeman, not Helena, and introduced him to both Pritchards, senior and junior. Pritchard senior was his father's lawyer, and had been for decades, which had been news to Will. He'd been a harmless-looking old man, except for the evil twinkle in his eyes.

Pritchard junior was to be Will's attorney for this affair, or so Will was told. The two younger men had rolled their eyes at each other, but Will's father was in ill health by then and to be humored on this subject. Will's mother had told him so, more firmly than she'd told him anything since Will had come back from the Klondike forty years before. She'd believed her husband's outlandish assertions. She'd told him she had proof it was true. And that he would have his own proof someday, too.

He'd chalked it up to the desperate belief of a woman who'd been head over heels in love with her husband for sixty years, and who knew she would soon lose the love of her life to death. Who was sure she would see him again, and she didn't necessarily mean in heaven. He'd wondered if his father had dementia, and if he really had been of sound mind when he'd signed that outlandish will. And when he insisted that Will sign another.

Will held his grandson in his arms, and stared down at the boy. Was this the so-called proof? This woman lying here, in her old-fashioned dress? Was she another time traveler, as his father claimed he was?

"Granddad." The boy was squirming again, and Will realized he was squeezing Chuck too tightly. It was surprisingly hard to loosen his arms.

"Granddad, she's going away."

Truly, she was. Fading was a better description. But at the last, her head turned. She stared up at him. He could almost see the sinter through her ever more-transparent body. Will's heart skipped one beat, then another. He knew those eyes, and that face, so much, much younger than the last time he'd seen them, and he realized, with an impact that almost knocked him over, that this was what his mother had meant by her proof. But she was frightened. Why? If she'd known, she shouldn't be. But he couldn't stand her fear, in spite of everything. So he winked at her. And his mother smiled up at him. Just before she winked out.

IV

Chuck was worn out by the time they'd made the short hike from the Grand back to their quarters, even with Will carrying him most of the way, and practically fell flat on his face into the sandwich Will made for him. Will put him to bed, even through the child's sleepy protests that he didn't need a nap.

Will wanted a nap, or more, himself. If it hadn't been for the fact that he could not close his eyes without seeing - his *mother*, dear God, lying there on the ground - he'd have curled up in a fetal position, as his father would have said, and conked out hoping to wake and find it was all a dream.

But he couldn't, although he tried. So he got up and dragged a chair out into the sunshine by the door of their quarters, and sat there watching the ravens and the jays quarrel the afternoon away, and both wished for and dreaded Karin's return.

She was so practical. She hadn't gone to Denver with them to see the Pritchards, but she'd listened to Will upon his return and told him there was no harm done. She'd even believed, a little, because of James. Well, so had he. A little.

But it was one thing to hear how his parents had found a little lost boy both he and Karin fell in love with on sight, whose existence had had no logical explanation. And another altogether to experience the phenomenon itself.

Time travel. *Dear God.*

The sun was low in the sky by the time their old truck came rattling down the road from West Yellowstone. Chuck came bouncing out of their quarters in his stocking feet at the sound.

"Grandmother!"

"Yes, that's Grandmother," Will told him. "Go put your shoes on, please, before she fusses at both of us."

Chuck pouted, but ran inside. He ran back out with one little boot in either hand just as the truck came around the corner of the building. Will stood and plunked the boy into his chair. "Put them *on*. Do not take another step till you do."

Instead the child dumped his boots on the chair and jumped back down. Will sighed and picked him up before going to open the truck door. Maybe Karin wouldn't notice -

She did, he could tell, the same way she noticed the way Chuck's blond hair was smashed down on one side. But it was Will she stared at. He hadn't thought to look in a mirror, but if he looked like he felt, he could understand why she was looking at him that way.

"Rough day?" was all she asked, but her eyes were eloquent.

He supposed that was one way to describe it. "You have no idea."

"We saw a ghost!" The nap had re-energized Chuck more than Will would have liked. He wriggled and grinned.

Karin tilted her head at Will and he gazed back helplessly at her. "Did you now?"

Will took a deep breath. If he couldn't count on his wife to keep him sane, he couldn't count on anyone. "Yes, we did."

She barely hesitated, bless her. "Well, then, help me bring in my shopping, and tell me all about it."

* * *

Will could no more have stopped Chuck from gabbling out the whole story than he could have put wings on the boy, thrown him into the air, and expected him to fly. Honestly, it was easier to let the five-year-old relish the outlandishness of it all than try to tell the wild tale to Karin himself. Will could tell she knew he felt that way, too, as she listened, glancing up at him occasionally, waiting for him to contradict the child. But Will didn't even have to correct any of the details.

Will wondered how much of this Chuck would remember by the time he was twenty, and if it would make a difference to what Charley insisted was to happen to Chuck at that age. If experience was anything to go by, and if, again, Charley was right about what had happened to James when he was the same age, then, no he wouldn't, and no, it wouldn't. Which was probably just as well.

Chuck finally ran down about the time Karin put supper on the table, and was too busy stuffing his little face after that to talk anymore. He listened to the adults, though, and Will was conscious of things he wanted, needed to say to Karin but couldn't in front of the boy. The long nap hadn't helped, either. It was well past dark before Chuck was tired enough to tuck back into bed, in proper pajamas this time. Will pulled another chair out in front of their quarters and helped Karin into it.

But before he could even open his mouth, she said, "Well, I guess that taught me to go off and leave the two of you on your own."

"You want to know the worst of it?" he asked her, feeling more than a bit wary.

She tilted her head at him. "That wasn't the worst?"

Here goes. "No, the worst of it is it's all true."

Her breath caught then let loose. She turned to look him in the eye, although how much she could see of his expression in the starlight was unclear to him. He certainly couldn't see much of hers. "Well. That's a relief."

"*What?*"

"Shh. You'll bring Chuck back out here." She had a point. Will counted to ten and let his breath out slowly.

"I've been expecting this ever since your mother warned me about the little - what was the word she used? Oh, yes. Oddities. The oddities in your family." Karin chuckled, still watching him, then went on, "She told me about her experience, about seeing the two of you, long before you went to Denver with your father. If it's any consolation, you frightened her as much as she scared you."

"She told you, but not me," Will said slowly.

"She told me I was the one who needed to know. Charley was vehemently against telling either of us, apparently. According to your mother, he was terrified of doing anything that might tear his loop in time. He wasn't big on trust, at least not about that. She said that if he could have figured out any way at all to manage the business without telling anyone else, he would have."

"I suppose I can understand. Still," he added, "I could have done with the warning."

"You'd have been looking over your shoulder for years now if you'd been warned."

"Is that why you didn't tell me?" He couldn't help feeling a bit accusatory.

"No, I didn't say anything because she asked me not to." Will started to expostulate, but she held up her hand. "She gave me good reason, love. She was deathly afraid you'd do something to prevent what happened, and that you'd rip the loop apart. She was pretty firmly convinced that she'd have died a captive of the Nez Perce if your father hadn't showed up when he did. But she also said she'd never have believed Charley no matter what he said if she hadn't seen for herself, and she was afraid that would rip them apart, too. I understand the not believing part. I wish I had proof myself."

Karin paused, and reached a hand over to his. Reluctantly, Will let her hold it, but he felt numb. She'd known. And she hadn't told him. Hadn't trusted him.

Then again, he hadn't believed, either. He'd gone along with his father's last wishes purely to humor him.

He realized suddenly that she was speaking again. "I think you needed to see, Will. To believe."

He snorted, almost in spite of himself. "You got that right."

"Do you forgive me?"

Will gazed into the eyes of the woman *he'd* loved for the last forty years. Everything he'd always wanted was in those bright blue eyes.

"You have to understand, Will. I was afraid, too."

He reached his free hand out to touch her face. Real, as the ghost of his mother had once been. "Afraid? Of what?"

"That if I told you I'd tear the loop."

"And if you had?"

"I'd have lost you," she told him simply, and kissed him.

AFTERWORD

Thank you for reading "Homesick." I hope you enjoyed it. Reviews help other readers find books. I appreciate all reviews, whether positive or negative.

Would you like to know when my next book is available? You can sign up for my new release email list at mmjustus.com, or follow me on on Facebook at https://www.facebook.com/M.M.Justusauthor on Twitter @mmjustus, or on Pinterest at http://www.pinterest.com/justus1240/

"Homesick" is a short story in the Time in Yellowstone Series, following the novels *Repeating History* and *True Gold*, and preceding the novel *Finding Home*. All are available in electronic and print versions from many vendors including your local bookstore.

If you would like to read an excerpt from *Repeating History*, please turn the page.

Repeating History

In 1959, 20-year-old college dropout Chuck McManis strolls the geyser boardwalks in Yellowstone National Park when an earthquake plunges him eighty years back in time, into the middle of an Indian war.

Into his personal past, too – his great-grandfather, his boyhood idol, but not a hero after all. Hapless Chuck needs instructions for sheer survival. He will not abandon Eliza Byrne, the woman who teaches him. But nothing matters if they never make it back to civilization. No matter when it could be.

CHAPTER 1

August 15, 1959

My summer school grades arrived the day after Granddad's funeral. I didn't bother opening them. I knew what was inside. Granddad would have appreciated the irony. I knew Dad wouldn't, and I was glad I'd got to the mail first. Dad was broken up enough over Granddad's death as it was. Although with him it wasn't easy to tell.

"It's time to go." He looked, as usual, like the accountant he is. Bland and smooth in his gray suit, white buttondown shirt, and navy blue tie.

"Sure." I wasn't wearing a suit, just jeans and a plaid shirt and my motorcycle boots. I didn't pat the pocket I'd stuffed the envelope in. Didn't want to draw attention to it. I pushed my glasses up and ran a hand over my dishwater blond buzz cut instead. Then tugged the sleeves of my leather jacket back down over my wrists. The curse of being a beanpole.

He looked me up and down and frowned but didn't say anything else as he locked the door behind us and led the way to his car. At least not until I went to my bike instead.

"You're not riding that *thing* to the lawyer's office."

I swung my leg over the Harley. "Sure I am."

"No, you're -" The rest of the rant, which I knew by heart, was lost in the rumble of the bike's engine. Music to my ears.

* * *

"And that's the last of it," Mr. Pritchard said, handing me Granddad's pocketwatch. So there had been something in the will for me, after all, as familiar as if I'd known it all my life. Which I had. I closed my hand around the smooth metal case, then stuffed it deep into the bottom of my jeans pocket. That was one thing I never wanted to lose. The lawyer straightened the sheaf of paper he was holding, and looked at Dad. I leaned back in my chair and stared out the window overlooking the street, wishing for a hamburger. Lunch had been a long time ago.

"I don't understand why he was so adamant about getting in here to see you two weeks ago," Dad said. "Nothing appears to have changed from the version he gave me last year."

Mr. Pritchard looked apologetic. "I should have said almost the last of it. The codicil he had me add at our last meeting doesn't have anything to do with the disposition of his property, but of his and your mother's remains."

That was creepy. Cremation was even worse than getting buried.

"I've bought a niche for both of them out at Cherry Hills," Dad said in that tone he has. *This is the way it is, period.*

Cherry Hills was the last place my grandparents would have wanted to end up, not that they were going to be able to tell the difference now. It's the ritziest cemetery in Denver, all carefully mowed lawns and fancy statuary. Besides, neither one of them liked Denver to begin with. Granddad had only given up and moved here to be closer to the Dad and me after Grandmother died and his health went downhill.

And when Dad had insisted. Granddad hadn't put up nearly as much of a fight about it as I'd thought he would, though.

"He was very specific about what he wanted done," Mr. Pritchard said, with almost exactly the same tone..

"Well, what *does*-" Dad broke off. I could almost see the blood draining from his face. *Why?* It couldn't be that bad. There's only so much you can do with a pile of ashes, after all. "No. Absolutely not."

Mr. Pritchard looked kind of surprised. "But I haven't even told you what he wanted done yet." Then he turned to me.

I could have sworn they'd completely forgotten I was there. God knows I was wishing I wasn't. What I wanted was to get on my bike and ride far away from this office, from Denver, from my grades burning a hole in my pocket, from the fact that Granddad was dead...

"Your grandfather wished for you to take their ashes back to Yellowstone and scatter them there. He wanted them left where he and your grandmother spent so much of their lives and were so happy together. I've arranged permission from the park service, and made reservations for you at the Old Faithful Inn for three nights starting tomorrow."

All I could think was *oh, my God. Really? Yes! Thank you thank you thank you, Granddad.* He couldn't have given me anything better if he'd tried. I sobered. Except to stay alive.

Mr. Pritchard paused, watching, smiling slightly at me. I could see Dad out of the corner of my eye, all the blood back in his face turning it red with – why was he so mad? Yeah, he didn't get it, wouldn't get it, but it wasn't that big a deal. Just four lousy days. In Yellowstone. Where I'd spent the best times with Grandmother and Granddad, growing up. A chance to get the hell out of here. "You should have plenty of time. If I understand correctly, you won't be going back to college this fall."

My jaw dropped, but before I could say anything, Dad took a deep breath. "And why not?" His fists were clenched on the arm of the chair, and he was past just red. He looked like he was going to explode. "What did you do this time, and why the *hell* didn't you tell me before it went this far?"

"I, uh." My tongue stuck in my throat. *Well, at least he knows now.* "I, uh, flunked Business Law. And Economic Analysis."

"*Again?*" He looked like he wanted to strangle me. I guess the only reason he didn't was where we were.

Mr. Pritchard was looking apologetic again. "I'm sorry. I thought you knew. I spoke out of turn."

I turned on him. Anything so I didn't have to look at Dad. "How the- How did you know about my grades? I just got them today."

His smile this time was almost a smirk. "Perhaps the two of you need to go home and talk this over."

Over my dead body. Which is what it was likely to be by the time Dad got done with me.

Dad apparently had the same idea, because he stood and grabbed me by the arm. I'm taller than he is, but he's got a helluva grip for a 62-year-old man. "Come on, son."

I glanced back at Mr. Pritchard as Dad dragged me out of the room. *Thanks a lot, Mister.*

* * *

I'm twenty years old. It's not like my father can stick me in my room and expect me to stay there. I packed up my duffel bag and snuck out that night while Dad was on the phone, talking to God knows who about God knows what. Well, not God knows what, although what Dad thought he could do to get Colorado State University to take me back again was sort of beyond me.

I spent what was left of the night at a diner, dozing with my coffee going cold on the table in front of me, and arrived at Pritchard's office at the crack of dawn the next morning. He got there pretty darned early himself, and he didn't seem to be surprised to see me. He handed me an envelope full of cash, gave me the paperwork for permission to pick up the ashes and the directions to the crematorium, which was one seriously strange place, and wished me good luck.

I was on the road to Yellowstone, duffel bag on the back of my bike, before rush hour even got started.

* * *

It was full dark and my legs were aching like a son of a gun by the time I came over the last rise to Old Faithful. I was so tired I was about to fall off the bike. But I'd made it.

Lights illuminated the valley below. The Inn, a huge pile of logs with windows, was surrounded by smaller buildings that made it look like the thing had had puppies, the river flowing between plumes of steam.

The road curved around past the low slung lodge and its cabins, past the visitor center, to the porte cochere, which had once protected fancy guests a long time ago, and now stood guard over people in jeans and pedal pushers towing their own suitcases.

I found a place to park the bike, and unhooked my duffle with one hand while swiping the road dust off my face with the other.

"Ooh," voices rose around me. "It's erupting."

I turned to watch with everyone else. I've seen Old Faithful go off dozens of times, but it had been a long time since Grandmother died, Granddad retired and I went off to college. I let my duffle drop to the ground and grinned. I could hear the roar over the people around me, through the memories in my head.

Dammit, I'd missed this place.

The geyser spent itself in a few minutes, and I watched, tickled, as people applauded. They always did, like the geyser was alive. Then, the show over, I picked up my bag and headed inside to claim my room.

* * *

I didn't bother with the Inn's dining room. Too pricey and too fancy. The store a few hundred yards away had a soda fountain. One of Granddad's and my favorite treats when Grandmother had gone to Jackson or West to go shopping for the day had been greasy hamburgers and fries at that fountain.

It was at the back of the store, a row of little round red stools and a metal counter, with a bunch of shiny chrome restaurant equipment and a pass-through behind it. As I approached it looked deserted. I hoped it wasn't closed. The rest of the store was busy with tourists buying souvenirs, but it was after the normal time most people ate supper.

Then, as I sat down on one of the stools, I saw this cute little rear end, round and sweet in a red and white striped skirt, bent over behind the counter.

"Hi," I said, and she shot up, straws spraying out of the box in her hand as she squeezed it.

"Oh! You startled me." She seemed to realize what she was doing to the box, and dropped it on the counter. Straws slithered everywhere, and she and I both made grabs for them.

Her front view was as good as the back. Nicely stacked, pretty face, brown curly hair escaping from a net.

She caught my eye, then fumbled for an order pad. "What can I get for you?"

I smiled at her. She smiled back. *Good.* "A hamburger, please. Fries. A Coke."

She scribbled it down. "It'll be just a minute." She turned to stick the order on the spindle in the pass-through window, and called out, "Joe! Order!"

Joe turned out to be Jo, a middle-aged woman wearing an apron shiny with grease who filled out her red-and-white dress a lot more solidly than my waitress did. She scowled at the order slip. "Grill's supposed to be closing."

"I know, Jo, but-"

"Yeah, you're a soft touch for a cute guy."

I smiled at her. The scowl melted from her eyes, although she tried to keep it on her mouth, and she slapped a burger on the griddle. I could hear it sizzle.

"Thanks, ma'am," I told her. "I've been on the road since six a.m."

"Yeah, yeah." Her gaze shot to the other end of the counter. "Loverboy at two o'clock."

The girl and I both turned to look. Her gaze fell, and she went back to picking up straws.

"Hey, Alice, what's a guy got to do to get some service around here?"

So much for my idea to ask her if she'd like to go for a beer later.

The guy was almost as tall as I am, and I'm six foot two, but he was a lot broader, and it looked like mostly muscle. He scowled at me. I shrugged and shoved my glasses up my nose. She'd been fair game till he showed up, but I wasn't going to muscle in on him now.

Reluctantly, as if pulled by strings, Alice made her way to the other end of the counter. As soon as she got within arm's length, he reached out and snagged her by the elbow, tugging her around the end of the counter so she practically bounced off of him. She sent an apologetic glance back towards Jo, who waved her off.

I sighed, and Jo turned towards me.

"Know anyplace a guy can get a beer around here?" I asked her. She smirked at me.

"Only place in the village licensed to sell liquor is the bar in the Inn, and they don't sell to underaged."

I ignored the dig since I was used to that kind of thing, swallowed my last french fry, and paid her.

Beer at the Inn would probably cost an arm and a leg, but what the hell. It had been one long day. There was enough money in Pritchard's envelope, and I'd earned it.

* * *

When I woke up it was pitch black and freezing. I was in my room, sprawled on top of the covers, with my head at the foot of the bed. I still had all my clothes on, which was a good thing or I probably would have frozen to death. I still had my boots on, as I discovered when one of them clunked against the log headboard. The vibration made my head rattle. I couldn't remember how I'd gotten there, but I must have managed it under my own steam. Nobody here I knew to do it for me. I sat up, and immediately decided the last couple of beers had been a mistake. My head rang, the room spun, and oh, man, I had to piss. Bigtime. Good thing the sink was handy, since the toilet was down the hall.

When I was done, I plunked myself back down on the bed and realized I wasn't going to get back to sleep anytime soon. The radiator was hissing, which didn't explain why I was freezing my ass off. Something was ruffling the curtains. I went over to look and discovered the window was open. That explained the temperature, at any rate. I closed it, and stayed to stare out into the night. The moon was full, shining off the river in the distance, illuminating the boardwalks and the trees, the occasional plume of steam. Not a soul to be seen. I pulled out Granddad's pocketwatch. Past eleven. Why not?

I hoisted my duffel onto the bed. The box was at the very bottom, tucked into one end where it had settled. I pried at the plastic lid with a fingernail. It refused to open. I sat for a minute, staring at it. Knife. I stood and began rooting through my pockets. That turned up nothing besides the watch but my room key and an unwrapped breath mint, growing a nice case of pocket crud. I brushed it off and stuck it in my mouth to get rid of it. Bad move. If I thought my mouth had tasted scuzzy before, it was twice as nasty now.

After I spit the mint into the garbage can, I found my pocketknife in the toe of my spare shoes, strangely enough. Gingerly I slid the blade along the seam of the box. With no warning, the lid snapped open and a poof of dust rose, straight into my face.

I snapped the lid back down, cussing. It wouldn't stay. "Okay. Okay." I set the box down on the little table next to the bed and backed away from it, swiping at my face, hoping I wasn't inhaling Grandmother and Granddad. Once the dust settled, I approached it again, and carefully closed the lid, feeling for the catch and pressing hard. This time it stayed. I let my breath out in a long whoosh.

I picked my pocketknife up off the floor, grabbed my leather jacket and the box, and headed out the door.

It was even colder outside, too cold for August even up here. And eerie, with no one around. I could hear sounds coming from the lodge across the road, music, thumps, and somebody's muffled laughter. They seemed very far away.

My momentum got me as far as the beginning of the boardwalk, where my boots sounded like somebody banging on a door out there in the middle of the night. I tried to straighten out my steps, but I guess I was still more toasted than I'd thought I was. No railings to lean on, either. I could have used one just then.

The bridge over the river echoed, too, but the water rushing underneath drowned some of that out. And it had railings. I stopped and watched the current for a while, leaning on the railing, but not too hard. I didn't want to topple over into the river, which seemed way too possible right then. Too much beer. *Sorry, Granddad.*

I took a better hold on the box. Time to move on. Granddad's will hadn't been all that specific about where to scatter the ashes, as long as it was in the park. I stopped and tried to think about it. Around Old Faithful seemed like kind of a cliché, and, anyway, I couldn't get close enough to the geyser anymore to scatter them properly. Not like when I was a kid and the only thing keeping a person from striding up and peering down the hole was his own good sense. Or his Granddad the park ranger. Besides, I was already on the other side of the river.

Observation Point seemed like a good idea until I started up the hill, grasping at tree branches and tripping over rocks in the dark. But I was halfway up before that dawned on me, and by then it was a matter of principle. So I kept going, and eventually I stood at the top, overlooking the whole valley in the moonlight.

The quiet was almost too much. No breeze, no sounds of animals – *they're all asleep, you idiot, everything with any sense is sound asleep* – no, wait a minute. I could hear splashing, muted by distance, and sank down on a rock to watch Old Faithful go off, as if it had waited for me to take my seat. I stared at it, spellbound, as if it was the first time I'd ever seen it. It certainly was the first time I'd ever had it all to myself, water spraying in the moonlight, steam clouds lifting into the sky.

Too soon, it was finished, and the night sounds took over again. A breeze picked up in the trees, and something chittered, then fell silent again. The scene below me looked like a painting. I felt like one of the early explorers, watching something no one would believe existed. The half-dozen remaining lighted windows of the inn might have been stars, the distant fires in the campground on the other side of the lodge might have belonged to an early expedition, or to old Colter himself. Or to the Indians. I shivered.

Here you are. Get it over with and get back to bed. I fished my pocketknife out and pried at the lid.

The box opened easily this time, and the dust wafted away into nothing in the slight breeze, more quickly than I expected. I shook out the last few bits. "Hope this does it for you, Granddad," I said into the night. "Miss you. Grandmother, too." I did. They were my real parents, the ones who'd taken me in and raised me after my mother died when I was born and Dad couldn't handle the whole situation. They were the ones who'd taught me who I was and who I wanted to be, who'd given me everything. Who'd understood me.

I didn't cry then. I don't cry much, at least not on the outside. But my chest was tight and my eyes burned, even though I knew I was doing the right thing. This trip felt like one last present they'd given me. Suddenly I was very glad things had worked out this way. In spite of having to sneak out on Dad. "You're home," I told them. "So am I. Thanks. I'll come back some day. I promise."

I tucked the box back under my arm and headed down the hill.

It was a fine night. Yeah, it was freezing, but my leather jacket kept me warm. The stars were shining like high beams against the sky and the beer was finally wearing off and I felt good about what I'd done. Sad, but good. I couldn't quite bring myself to go back inside. Not yet. To go back inside was to say the whole thing was over. I had three nights, so I didn't have to go back and face my real life yet – *this is real life, dammit.* Flunking out of college was what felt like a dream right now. Or a nightmare. So I didn't go in. I got myself down the trail to the valley, and decided to take a little stroll instead. It wasn't likely I'd ever have the place to myself like this again, unless I got drunk for the next two nights, which didn't feel like a bad idea now that the hangover was wearing off.

I'd wandered a ways down the path when the ground began to vibrate under my feet.

I looked up from my thoughts to find myself in front of Grand Geyser. I grinned. The tremors meant I might get to watch another eruption before I went back in. I sat down crosslegged on the planks to wait and watch.

The moon gleamed on the pool under the boardwalk, the ripples growing into small waves as the vibrations magnified. A splash, another splash, this one bigger than the first, a chugging racket that sounded like the propellers on an airplane about to take off...

The earthquake, it had to be an earthquake, hit like a giant pounding a sledgehammer. The boardwalk – bounced. With me on it. It was like riding a bucking bronco. I grabbed the edge of the boards, and hung on. Grand's pool was churning like a crazy thing now. Water hit me on the back, the heat soaking through my jacket and shirt.

Then it all stopped. "That was a helluva ride," I said into the suddenly still darkness, the moon glimmering off the still sloshing pool. My thumb hurt. I held it up a few inches from my nose. A splinter was lodged under the nail. I grasped it between my teeth and yanked it out. Tugged the tail of my shirt out to stanch the blood. And stared around.

Everything seemed to be holding its breath. Not a bit of movement, except the water draining under my feet. Not a sound, except for the now-fading hiss of the runoff. I took a deep breath and started to get up.

That's when the big one hit.

CHAPTER 2

One second I was halfway to standing up, with some vague idea of making a mad dash back to my bike to get the hell out of there, the next I was flat on my face, hanging onto the boardwalk again like it was my last friend. I rolled partway over to get a better grip and stared up, and up, and up, as Grand exploded less than 20 feet from my face. The ground shook again, water shot up 100 feet, 150 feet, 200 feet, I don't know how high it went. All I know is I'd seen Grand go off plenty of times every summer when I was a kid, and I'd never seen it like this.

The water, filled with chunks of stuff, rocks, bits of wood, crap I couldn't identify if I'd wanted to, was landing all around me like a rain of missiles. I couldn't make my legs work. Only when a big gout of the backsplash hit me full in the face did I even try to curl up to protect myself. I couldn't see. My glasses were covered in dirty water and my head was buried in my arms. I didn't want to look. I never wanted to see a geyser again as long as I lived.

The ground rolled again underneath me like a ship's deck in a storm. Big, lazy, sickening. Then it jerked. Hard. I felt myself flying through the air, a piece of the now-splintered boardwalk still clutched in my fists. Something like a club smashed into the back of my head. I saw stars behind my tightly shut eyelids. And then I saw nothing at all.

* * *

The ground was warm and still and wet beneath me as I came to, the air icy above. I tried to open my eyelids and couldn't. I reached up to touch my face. It was sticky, and so were my hands. And the rest of my skin. My clothes rasped as I moved, and I was afraid to touch my glasses.

I reached my tongue out and licked my lips, then jerked it back in. Sulfur and brimstone would taste like that. I took my glasses off, and carefully wiped my eyes with my finger. I might as well not have bothered. The steam was still as thick as butter. Slowly I climbed to my feet. On the bare ground. Where was the boardwalk? I stared at the wet, cloudy glasses. *Don't scratch them up, then what will you do?* I wiped them carefully, my hands shaking, half a dozen splinters in my palms from clenching the wood during the explosion. I shoved a hand through the stiff hair on the back of my head, then brought it forward to look at it. No blood. I reached back again. Just a tender spot. A big one.

I inventoried the rest of me. Nothing else seemed to be damaged. I stank of sweat and mud and sulfur, my head pounded, and my hands hurt, but otherwise I was okay. I absentmindedly began pulling the splinters out as the steam drifted around me.

Dad will never believe this. I wonder if anyone will.

At last I could see a little. Something that could have been a tree, tall and dark and shadowy, swam into view a few yards away, and I took a couple of steps towards it, the ground echoing beneath my feet. *You're walking on the crust, you idiot.* I stopped, frozen, every warning Granddad had drilled into me running through my head like a broken record.

"People have died stepping off the boardwalks, young man. Scalded to death, the meat boiled off their bones." He'd been trying to keep me from running down the boardwalks, which made a wonderful thundery noise. At seven, the idea of falling in had been creepily fascinating, not terrifying. It was terrifying now.

"Animals, too?" I'd asked, and Granddad had taken me to a spring where a buffalo skull still gleamed whitely in the clear depths. I could see myself in the bottom of one of those springs right now, cooking till there was nothing left of me but pale bones.

* * *

But I couldn't stand here all night. Someone would find me eventually, but *when?*

The ground around me looked like it had been torn up with a fire hose, all gullies and bare earth. I stood very, very still staring at the tree a few long yards away, not at all sure what was holding me up where I was, until it dawned on me that a tree has roots that go deep. I'd be safe there.

I took a deep breath, and a step forward. The ground held. Another, and another, and I was on grass. A few feet more, and I was leaning on that tree, breathing hard.

Now what? I peered through my still-smudged lenses. A few more trees loomed through the steam in the moonlight, but that was about it. The way back toward the inn was all geyserite and no boardwalks. The only solid ground lay uphill.

I tried sidling along the slope, which didn't work. I gave up and headed uphill. The valley was behind me. As soon as I got to the top I'd circle around. How lost could I get?

Pretty lost, in the dark, with the ground covered with trees like a giant's pick-up sticks. The moon went down, and I didn't even notice it till I stopped to try to orient myself. I was pretty sure I was headed towards Observation Point, where I'd scattered my grandparents' ashes less than one long hour before. I'd have to run into the trail. Eventually. Then I'd know where I was.

It was three in the morning, according to Granddad's pocket watch, by the time I realized I wasn't going to find anything. Not till light anyway. The trail had to be somewhere nearby, but unless it had been completely destroyed by the earthquake -- *how could an earthquake blow away an entire mile-long trail?* -- I was a lot more lost than I wanted to admit.

It couldn't be that much longer till first light. Three hours? Maybe four? I sank down onto a fallen log and rubbed more mineral grit off my face, then tried, and failed, to get up again.

The hell with it. I slid down the side of the log until I hit the ground, leaned back on it, and closed my eyes.

They popped open again less than a minute later. The noise sounded like an entire army platoon crashing around in the brush. A rescue party?

When no one knew you were out here?

Maybe someone else had gone exploring in the middle of the night. *No. Only you could be that stupid.*

The noise stopped, suddenly enough to leave my ears ringing. I sat, the adrenaline sluicing through my veins, my body too tired to react to it, and waited for something else to happen. Nothing did. A rock under my butt, a branch in my back. I shifted, got a little more comfortable, which wasn't saying much. The hours crept by. I kept dozing off, in spite of everything, only to be jerked awake by the strangest sounds. A chirp. A rustle. A weird scraping noise that turned out to be a branch rubbing up against the trunk of another tree. A breeze picked up, reminding me my clothes were still damp, then died. I started to shiver. I wrapped my arms around my knees, propped my chin on them, and waited.

* * *

Light came eventually, a faint gray glow that enabled me to see, rather than sense, the trees, if only as darker gray globs that became clearer and clearer against pink and yellow.

At least I know where the hell east is now. Sort of.

"Even in the summer the sun doesn't rise directly east," Granddad had said. "Do you know why?"

"Because we're not on the equator," my nine-year-old self had told him. I'd been as proud to be able to pronounce the big word as I'd been to know what it meant.

"That's right. So you have to adjust for it."

Knowing where east was gave me only part of the solution. I didn't know how far I'd come last night, but I'd spent more time weaving through lodgepole pine thickets than I had going forward. For all I knew I'd been wandering in circles.

But I should have been able to hear other people by now. The lodge was only half a mile away. I pulled Granddad's pocketwatch out again, and wound it this time. Seven a.m. Not too early for breakfast. My stomach growled. The thought had me striding down the hill before I could stop myself. Eggs and bacon and coffee...

The hole must have belonged to some little critter, but it caught my foot like I'd stepped into a bear trap. I went down with a thud that made my aching head ring and my bruised butt reverberate. Tears sprang to my eyes. The yell jerked out of me. "Uncle, dammit!"

Nobody responded. Not that I'd have heard them. I was too wrapped up in my own physical agony to pay any attention. Every bump and bruise from yesterday woke up and started screaming in sympathy. My ankle hurt like hell, and pulling it out of the hole told me walking on it any time soon wasn't going to be a great idea. Even if the little voice in the back of my head told me it probably wasn't broken.

Nothing felt like a great idea then except cradling my ankle and cursing. Except I couldn't even think of cusswords adequate for this situation.

"Uncle, dammit," I said again, not yelling this time, and put my forehead down on my knee.

I sat there for quite a while.

* * *

The sun was way above the trees before I managed to get myself up and moving again. The little voice in the back of my head had been right -- the ankle wasn't broken. I really didn't want to try to walk on it, though. Slowly I rose, pulling myself up on a nearby tree. I found a piece of deadfall a few feet away. It wasn't quite long enough for a walking stick, and it wasn't all that sturdy, but it was better than nothing.

* * *

I never did find the Observation Point trail. Or the one I'd made coming up the hillside. I'd have thought I'd thrashed a trail obvious enough for Mr. Magoo to find it, but apparently not.

I couldn't find the river, either. Or the lodge.

The whuffing noise behind me almost made me land flat on my face as I spun around. *What the-*

All I registered at first was rough black fur and shiny little eyes. The bear stopped dead about six feet in front of me. I could smell its breath, rotten, puffing into my face. I didn't even realize I was holding my own till it came out in a whoosh.

It wasn't that big, I told myself, a half-grown black bear, which didn't seem to matter right then. It didn't look ticked, just curious, but for all I knew that could have meant it was sizing me up for lunch.

It went up on his hind legs. Not that big. *Uh-huh.* My knees almost gave out from under me.

Its head began to sway back and forth. I watched, almost hypnotized. I couldn't run. My ankle wasn't going to let me. Even if it had, I don't think I could have moved.

Suddenly Granddad's voice came back to me again. "If it's a black bear, not a grizzly, you can try to scare it off. Wave your arms. Yell. Make racket."

I hope you're right. I took a deep breath. "Yah-yah-yah! Go 'way, bear!" I took my stick and whanged it against a tree, then feinted with it like it was a sword. "Yah! Scat!" I stomped my good foot.

The bear dropped back down. It lowered its head. *Oh, no. Thanks, Granddad.* "Yah, bear! Shoo! Go 'way!" I yelled as loud as I could, brandished the stick, which promptly caught on a branch and almost knocked me off my feet. I jerked it loose and, purely by accident, I whacked that bear right on top of his head.

It wasn't a hard hit, but it sure got his attention. I thought at first he was going to charge me, but he just glared at me, turned away and lumbered off into the trees.

I sagged against a pine, which bent nearly to the ground, taking me, and my ankle, with it.

It took another while for the pain to subside enough for my growling stomach to get me moving again. I pulled myself upright on a sturdier tree this time, and took a tentative step. Nope, not broken, just banged up. I took one step, then another, leaning on my stick, examining every single spot before I put each foot down.

* * *

I don't remember how long I walked, or how far. I do remember watching the sun go down and the light fade, and the sky grow dark and patterned with stars. I remember finally stopping again and curling up in a hollow next to a small hot spring, listening to the strange sounds of the forest in the night.

I was too tired and hungry to care about them anymore. If I was eaten by wild animals, at least I wouldn't have to die of terminal embarrassment when a rescue party found me. If they found me.

A long, ululating howl broke the churning of my thoughts. *That's one big coyote.* It came again, then a second and a third, blending in a series of harmonics that made the hair on my arms stand on end. *Big pack of coyotes.* But it couldn't be anything else. Wolves had been gone from the park for decades.

Had a pack escaped the slaughter? How? The wails echoed around me, over me, through my veins and inside my bones. I shuddered in sympathy, my breathing shallow. The pack sang for what seemed like hours, stopping as if only to make the silence echo their voices. I sat, unable to close my eyes because of what I would see with those sounds as a backdrop.

Once, when I was nine, back when my father was still battling the grandparents for me, Dad took me to the opera. "There's more to life than hiking in the woods," he told me. Finally he'd tempted me with dragons, Fafner in Wagner's opera, which did interest me. So much that it gave me nightmares for weeks. Tonight, I thought, tonight of all nights Fafner will be back, howling like a wolf and chasing me through the night.

The wolves weren't close, even my terrified backbrain knew that, but it didn't seem to matter. I watched steam rise from that little circle of hot water, and it looked like Fafner's mouth spitting smoke and fire. I listened to the opera, coming, it seemed, from all around me. And I shivered, in spite of the heat from the spring, and waited the night out.

* * *

I swear it took years for the sky to lighten. Even longer for the day to penetrate the thicket of lodgepole pine and brush I was buried in. The wolves had quieted some time back, to be replaced by birdsong and the recognizable sounds of small critters coming out of their refuges in the safety of early morning. A jay screeched overhead. A chipmunk popped out from under a downed tree and stared at me before skittering off somewhere.

I grabbed my bear-bonking stick and levered myself up, every muscle aching. I put my right foot down and almost bit my lip through to keep from yelling at the pain.

Wonderful. Now what?

I should have thought of my bug bandanna in the first place. Standard equipment for the motorcycle, and it was still in the pocket of my leather jacket. I took my boot off and wrapped my ankle with it. Never thought I'd be all that grateful for first aid classes, but Granddad told me I'd be a fool if I didn't take them when I had the chance. When I stood up, I could put enough weight on my foot to walk with the stick.

If only I knew which way to go. I picked a direction at random and started walking.

It wasn't easy. The lodgepole pines were like jackstraws waiting to trip me up. I'd thought I was in good shape, but I was banged up and I hadn't eaten for almost 48 hours. And I was *thirsty*. I wanted coffee. And aspirin, for my ankle as well as my head. And bacon and eggs and a Danish or three. Then I wanted to go back to my room, turn out the lights, and go fetal for about twelve hours.

I trudged on, working my way through the trees. I hadn't gone that far, when suddenly the ground ended. I came to an abrupt stop. Ahead of me the hillside fell away sharply, the forest opening up to a broad view that somehow seemed strangely familiar. I leaned on my bear bonker and stared out at it.

It looked like the view I'd seen the night before as I watched Old Faithful play in the moonlight, but it couldn't be the same. No signs of civilization decorated this panorama. No boardwalks, no benches. I inhaled sharply. No buildings. No store. No Inn.

I shook my head. I must have wandered farther than I thought. There were several geyser basins in the back country. It could be one of them.

A small rock rolled out away from my foot and gathered momentum as it bounced down the steep slope in front of me. I backed away before I followed it.

I could see the headlines now: "Among the missing from the earthquake at Yellowstone, the grandson of a former district ranger..." At least Granddad wasn't still around to be embarrassed on my behalf.

I sank down on a log with my chin in my hands, not wanting to think at all.

Gradually I became aware I was staring into a bush full of tiny dark blue berries. Almost without thinking, I reached out and pulled half a dozen from their stems. They gave readily, the branch bouncing back to its place. I sniffed them and set one between my teeth.

Oh, God. Huckleberries. The juice exploded across my tongue like a waterfall. I stuffed the rest of the handful into my mouth and surged forward, filling my hands, my mouth, juice dribbling down into the stubble on my chin.

It took a dozen of them to make a decent mouthful, and there were hundreds of decent mouthfuls within my reach. I didn't stop until my stomach started to make bad noises, and almost not even then, but

I didn't want to throw up. I flung myself down on the ground, wiping my blue mouth with my equally blue fingers. "Breathe, stupid. Breathe."

The huckleberries, so beautiful and tangy just minutes before, now felt like a geyser inside me, ready to erupt.

I swallowed, hard, and lay still. Gradually, the bubbling and sloshing slowed. I made it up to the stump again and stared at the ravaged bushes in front of me. *What did you expect, you idiot? Go hungry for two days, then gorge yourself on berries. You'll be lucky if you don't spend the next two days with your face in the toilet.* So to speak. Ignoring the gurgling in my stomach, I stood up and continued the day's ever more random hunt for civilization.

* * *

I don't remember if it was the fourth or fifth day that I almost fell in a spring by accident, then did it deliberately. I still itched from the geyser, and days of walking had only added layers of grime. It was too hot in the pools, but I wandered down a runoff channel, hoping for some sympathetic mojo. It would be my luck the minute I stripped someone would show up.

I found the perfect spot, at the perfect temperature. It was barely deep enough to wet my ankles, but even the sulfur reek couldn't possibly have been any worse than my own.

I stripped. Glanced around, saw nothing but a couple of curious squirrels, and stepped in.

I promptly landed on my bruised, bare butt, and sat, catching my breath, my backside screaming, as the reverberations died away.

Carefully I rearranged myself on the slippery geyserite, and began to wash. The water was warm and silky. The sun beamed down on my naked back, and I splashed and scared the squirrels away and had a helluva time.

"Granddad, why can't I swim in the hot springs?"

"Because they'll boil the meat off your bones." Granddad stood on the boardwalk at Morning Glory Pool. I rode his shoulders. I was six, I think.

"They're not *all* hot, are they?"

"Most of 'em are." He leaned his head around and looked up at me quizzically. "Besides, I didn't think you liked baths. You like rotten eggs?"

I made a face and felt Granddad's chuckle vibrate. "If I can throw 'em."

He swung off down the boardwalk onto the trail, his boots thumping. I settled myself more comfortably. "You're almost too heavy for me anymore, boy."

But I knew that wasn't true. I'd never be too heavy for Granddad.

I stayed in the runoff channel till my fingers turned pruny and my shoulders started to tingle from too much sun. Climbing out turned out to be at least as slippery as getting in had been, though. I was pulling my underwear back on when I heard something. I stood up too suddenly and almost tripped over my own feet. Was that a voice? I waited for a minute, then looked down at myself, underwear halfway up my legs, buck naked otherwise, and scrambled for the rest of my clothes. The second I had my boots laced, I was off up the hill, my shoulders scratching under my shirt.

"Stop, you idiot. Listen." Silence. Not even birds. Then the sound came again. I slumped. I looked up at the slope where a pine had fallen, victim to some damage or other. There wasn't room, in the dense lodgepole forest, for it to fall all the way to the ground, and it leaned against another tree. As I watched, the wind caught it again, and the sound, more like a violin bow scraping against the strings now that I knew what it was, wound through the air towards my ears.

I looked down at my shaking hands. *So that's what hallucinations are like.* No, that's what hallucinations could be like, if I didn't find something besides berries to eat pretty soon.

My mouth watered. My legs quivered in front of me. Suddenly the time I'd spent in the runoff channel seemed wasted. Stupid.

I wanted to cry. *It's only been a few days. Granddad would be ashamed of you.* I wiped my face on the back of my hand, and went looking for something. Anything. Nothing.

* * *

A day or two, or three, later, I had another run-in with a bear. I guess he wasn't pleased with me eating his huckleberries, because I ended up in a tree, swaying like it was in a high wind, and I thought I was going to land square on top of him if he didn't knock the tree over first. The world went gray around the edges for the first time then, and I closed my eyes and hung on, and kept them closed until long after I couldn't hear anything anymore.

The tree did dump me flat on my face when I tried to get down. A stick on the ground gave me a poke close enough to my eyes to scare me out of the fugue I'd been in.

I got up and dragged myself on. My ankle was better, but my feet felt like lead weights. The sun beamed down through the trees like my own personal oven. The pines oozed sap and all the little sounds of dusk and dawn were still.

Except me, who sounded like an elephant, at least to my own ears. An elephant whose vocabulary would have gotten me in dutch with my dad. Well, Dad wasn't here, and I was. Dammit.

I was getting weaker from lack of food, and I knew it. Stumbling more often, halting to let my head stop spinning, watching my hands shake every time I exerted myself more than a few steps.

At least I wasn't all that hungry anymore. The runs had petered out, mainly because I hadn't given my bowels anything *to* run, but I had nightmares about huckleberry seeds sprouting and growing through my intestines. Like the kid who's afraid to eat watermelon for fear he'll swallow a seed and have vines coming out his nose because that's what some smart-aleck older kid told him.

It was hard to think of anything in terms of common sense. I'd long since given up on trying to do anything that would have made Granddad proud of me. Or wasting energy cussing him out for getting me into this mess. The fact that I was still alive would have to do.

I came up over the crest of the hill and stared down at the valley below me with a sense of déjà vu that almost knocked me off my feet.

Far below, in a billow of steam, a geyser was playing. I'd have sworn it was Old Faithful, with its broad flat mound. But nothing else looked the same at all. No Inn, no boardwalks, no parking lots full of cars, no roads... No nothing, except steam and the splashing of water I could hear as the wind carried the sound up to my disbelieving ears. Not even any debris from the earthquake. It was as if no one had ever been here before.

As I watched, my mouth hanging open and my eyes damp, Old Faithful -- it had to be Old Faithful -- reached the peak of its eruption and began to subside. A few minutes later it was finished but for a lingering plume of steam. I sat down, and, I hate to admit it, began to cry.

* * *

At last I took a deep breath and sniffed, hard, and wiped my face on the torn sleeve of my shirt.

Then I dared to look up again.

The angle I was looking down from wasn't familiar, but I couldn't figure out why. I stared down on the scene till my eyes burned, mapping everything in my head, mumbling aloud as I noticed each surreal anomaly.

"That's where the lodge should be," I murmured, studying a point to the right of Old Faithful. "There's that big rock you can see from the dining room windows." That sidetracked me for a minute as hamburgers and French fries and milkshakes danced in front of my eyes. I swiped at them with a grimy hand and kept looking.

"There's where the visitor center is, where Granddad used to work." That spot was open, part of the meadow the Firehole River coursed through. As I watched, a buffalo wandered leisurely through it, stopping to jerk up a big mouthful of grass, stems dripping from his teeth. I could almost hear him chewing from where I sat.

"And the road." I lifted a finger and traced where it should have come up the valley from the west, past Biscuit Basin and Morning Glory Pool, along by Grotto Geyser, which was churning away at the moment, and around to where I had somehow managed to hallucinate Old Faithful Inn into oblivion.

It was all too real. Too much. It was morning before I came to myself again.

* * *

I woke to the sun in my eyes. I picked a couple of stray pine needles out of the fuzz on my face, pulled off my glasses and sat up, leaning back on one hand and rubbing my eyes with the other before I put them back on. Something had waked me. I couldn't place it, couldn't see it, couldn't even feel anything but the normal dizziness. I lay back down and stretched, then slowly climbed to my feet, leaning on the stump for support.

Down in the valley, nothing had changed. Or, nothing had changed back. Everything seemed so ordinary, and yet so un-ordinary. I felt like Rip van Winkle.

The shadows moved across my face, the sun blinding me momentarily before it moved on, half a hundred times. Old Faithful, living up to its name, erupted, once, twice, three times? I wasn't keeping count.

The sun had moved far enough to quit flashing in my eyes as it shifted when I heard the sounds. Thin and wispy, at first I thought my senses were playing tricks on me again. Then I thought, birds? Squirrels? The sound of a neigh brought me bolt upright, then to my feet. I stood, swaying.

A trail of dust, like it had been thrown up behind a car on a dirt road, lofting into the sky behind what? I couldn't see for the thicket of trees. I grabbed my stick and plunged headlong down the hill.

Three steps and I was bounding, two more, and nothing could have slowed me down. Three bounds after that, my foot caught on a branch, and I went sprawling. I hauled myself up, swiped the blood from my streaming nose on my shirtsleeve, and ran on.

The slope leveled out not much farther on. Springs and pools and bare ground signaling thin crust were everywhere. I stopped a moment to wipe my bloody nose again, and to breathe while I looked for the dust trail. It was gone.

I landed on the ground with a hollow thump. It told me maybe I shouldn't be sitting on that spot, but I didn't much care.

I shook myself. Had I imagined the dust cloud, too? My nose finally stopped bleeding, although it ached like a son of a gun. I fell back against the hard ground and shivered, trying to think. It took all my effort, not only mentally, but physically.

It was then it hit me. If all this was a hallucination, it wasn't going to be any good to go looking for that dust. If I wasn't hallucinating, then I wasn't where I thought I was in the first place. Screwed both ways.

But if this was real, what *happened*? And if this wasn't real, where was I and how did I get back out of this rabbit hole?

Questions chased themselves around in my brain like a dog chases its tail. I had way too many of them, and not a single answer to be found, anywhere, at any price.

It was then I began to hear the voices.

I went stock still and strained my ears. Yes, voices, drifting in on the breeze, faint, but unmistakably human.

I couldn't make out the words. Men's voices, baritone and tenor, and one shrill soprano. They gradually got louder, then one of the geysers went off, and I couldn't hear anything for a few minutes. I wondered if they'd still be there.

A woman's voice, the words suddenly as clear as if she were declaiming onstage. "She's just a little girl, William. You're too hard on her."

My head jerked up. That had to be real.

The deep-voiced man was speaking again. I homed in on the sound, and began to walk. Fast. Well, run, actually. Carefully. Sort of.

Who am I fooling? Those were the first human voices I'd heard in I don't know how many days. I stumbled, legs wobbly, head spinning, across the meadow towards them.

CHAPTER 3

The smell was the next thing to hit me. Frying bacon. I didn't even stop to wonder what these people were doing cooking bacon out in the middle of the wilderness. I kept going, thinking, if I was thinking at all, of food and people. Civilization. Somebody who could get me to a telephone, or a ride back to the inn and my bike. Food.

The voices stopped. I stumbled, and almost did land flat on my face. But I couldn't stop. I leaped like a deer, and cleared the last three jackstrawed logs with one jump.

And stopped, staring.

Twelve sets of eyes stared back at me. Six of them were human. The other six sets belonged to horses, which after a moment went back to cropping the grass in the clearing. The six people sat around a campfire, tin plates in hand, bacon and big, misshapen biscuits piled high, coffee steaming from enameled mugs. My mouth watered. I stepped forward.

"Are you lost, young man?" The woman's voice was the same as I'd heard a few minutes before. *Not a hallucination, by God.* She stood and smiled at me.

I couldn't find my voice.

"Looks like he is, Mrs. Byrne," said one of the four men.

The sixth, much younger, person jumped up, her grin wide. "Cat got your tongue, mister?"

"He looks worn out." Mrs. Byrne reached out. I took another step forward, then another, and before I knew it, I was sitting on a log, a plateful of steaming bacon and biscuits with honey in my lap, and my hand wrapped around one of those thick enameled mugs full of coffee.

I glanced around once, at their smiling faces, and dug in.

It was the best food I'd ever eaten. Better than Grandmother's cooking, better than any fancy restaurant I'd ever been to, better than anything this side of heaven. I know I made a pig of myself. I couldn't help it. Mrs. Byrne kept filling my coffee mug from the metal pot sitting at the edge of the fire, and, at her gesture, one of the men refilled my plate. Twice. I didn't stop eating until my stomach started cramping. I held my breath, willing the food to stay down where it belonged.

From one extreme to the other. It was a trade I was willing to make.

Over the churning I heard laughter, and the voices of my rescuers.

"Musta been lost a while to be that hungry."

"He's gonna be sick." This, from the little girl, made me raise my head.

"No, I'm not."

She giggled. "Yes, you are. You're green under your beard."

I reached up and felt the scraggle of fur on my chin. No, not just stubble, but a full-fledged beard.

Then, in spite of everything I could do to stop it, my stomach heaved, and I proved the little girl right, as I jerked to my feet and ran for the bushes.

* * *

I sat on a stump for a few minutes afterwards, feeling stupid and dizzy.

A voice behind me made me jump. "Waste of good food."

"Yeah," I said, looking up. A tall, clean-shaven fellow in a maroon cotton shirt, suspenders, and canvas trousers, his boots grimy and his face forbidding, went on. "Mrs. Byrne wants to know if you need any help."

He obviously didn't care if I did. "I'm okay." I stopped. No, I wasn't. I needed these people to get back to civilization, whether they liked it or not. "I could use a ride."

"Tenderfoot," he muttered, and turned back to camp. I got up and followed him.

The expressions that met me back at the campfire were no less curious than they had been the first time, but I was readier to face them, more or less.

"Sorry about that," I muttered, my face hot under the layers of dirt.

The older woman reached for the coffeepot and the mug I'd been using. I shook my head with a grimace, and then took my first good look at her. Her clothes were so peculiar it took me a while to get to her face. She was wearing a skirt, long enough the hem almost dipped into the coals at the edge of the fire when she leaned forward, her free hand scooping them back at the last moment. Her dress was blue, her eyes brown, and her hair, scraped back in a bun, was mahogany. She had freckles across the bridge of her nose and on her cheeks.

She wasn't exactly pretty, her features were too strong. She couldn't have been much older than I was, but she wore a gold band on her left hand.

A loud clearing of throats stopped my perusal. I jerked my head around.

"What's your name, boy?" said an older man who looked like he could eat me for breakfast.

"Chuck McManis." I couldn't help myself. I turned back to Mrs. Byrne. "Why are you dressed like that? Aren't you afraid you'll set it on fire?"

She stared at me. The little girl giggled, then looked to my right and sobered up. I looked to my right and closed my mouth.

"What did you say to my wife?"

Oh, no. I didn't know what it was I'd said, but that was beside the point. "Uh." I tried to breathe. "Uh."

His arm swung back, his hand in a fist. I braced myself for a blow that never came.

"William!" The woman leaped to her feet and across to her husband. "Don't you dare hit that poor young man. Can't you tell he's half delirious?"

It sure felt like it. I swayed and the world went black.

I came to sometime later with a headache the size of the Grand Canyon, as Granddad would have said. I was flat on my back on a narrow cot, a blanket over my feet and a pillow under my head. Over my head was dark canvas, the sun a vivid green spot through it. I squeezed my eyes shut, my head pounding.

The tent flap rattled, and I opened them a slit. The little girl peeked in. "He's awake!" I winced as the drummer in my head hit the cymbals.

"Anna, hush." Mrs. Byrne said. "Go find your bonnet. You'll look like a Red Indian soon."

Anna grimaced, but then she vanished, and I relaxed again. The canvas cot felt like a feather mattress under my body. *I* felt like someone had decided to beat me up with a baseball bat.

The back of my head was tender again, as I discovered when I touched it. My stomach and I had reached an uneasy truce -- it wouldn't throw up again if I didn't try to stuff it again -- but I still didn't trust it. My nose hurt. And every muscle in my body felt pummeled.

At least my ankle felt better. Maybe it was the competition.

I couldn't stay in here forever, though, in spite of how good the idea sounded. I leaned up on one elbow and watched the tent swim drunkenly around me. Then again, maybe I could.

The tent flap rattled again. It wasn't the irritated William, or the chirpy Anna, but one of the other men, younger and annoyingly cheerful as he grinned at me. I grimaced at him. He disappeared.

Not for long, though.

A few minutes later he returned and held the flap open. The light made me wince for a moment before it was blocked by the figure of Mrs. Byrne. She smiled at me. "Are you feeling any better?"

I tried out a smile in return. She ducked into the tent, a small bucket of water in one hand, a bandanna-wrapped bundle in the other, and a cloth draped over her shoulder.

Uh-oh.

She set the bucket down and sat on the edge of the cot.

"Mr. Byrne," she added, "is off to see if he can shoot some game to add to the larder. I told him if he was so worried about you eating all our supplies, he could go do something about it." She pulled the cloth down from her shoulder and wet one corner of it in the bucket.

I reached for it as she aimed it towards my face, but she pulled it back.

"You don't have to do that."

"You can't see what you're doing. Here." She handed me a cold biscuit. "Eat that. Slowly, please."

She reached out with the cloth again. I took a bite and closed my eyes for a moment in appreciation.

I could feel her fingers under the damp cloth. They were slender, but warm and strong as she scrubbed at the inground dirt and crusted blood.

She wasn't much older than I was. Why she was married to that old man was more than I wanted to know. He was a complete jerk. She, on the other hand, wasn't all that beautiful on first glance, but still. I watched her as she put some kind of ointment on my scrapes and felt around the back of my head for the lump I already knew was swelling.

"You conked yourself a good one," she said. "I imagine it hurts." Her smile was pretty, no doubt about that. It went all the way to her eyes this time.

Right then I couldn't have told her one way or the other whether it hurt or not. All I wanted to do was ask her-

"He's gone hunting? In a national park?" I swear that wasn't what I thought I was going to say.

Her smile melted away, the spell broken. "Yes."

"Doesn't he know it's illegal? He could get in a lot of trouble for that. How'd he get into the park with a gun, anyway?"

She shook her head, the look in her eyes confirming her diagnosis of delirium, and went back to her work, but she didn't answer me, just kept her eyes down and her hands busy.

I put a hand on her wrist. Gently, she shook it off.

"Can't you tell me what's going on here?"

Her eyes, full of pity, met mine again.

"How long were you out there?"

I stopped and thought. It made my head hurt. "A week, maybe? But-"

"What happened to your companions?"

"Companions?"

"Were you out there *alone*?" She rose to her feet, gathering her stuff. "Maybe William was right."

"Right about what?" I asked her back.

"You are a fool."

The tent flap fell behind her, and I started to flop back on the cot, then thought better of it. I lay back slowly, carefully settling my sore head, and took another bite of biscuit.

* * *

She didn't come back all afternoon. I had given up trying to figure out what was going on and was unsuccessfully trying to get some more sleep when Anna stuck her head in and told me there was food if I wanted it. My stomach growled. She laughed and disappeared.

Slowly I sat up. The world didn't spin, and my stomach didn't heave. I got to my feet and went out.

The day had ended while I'd been trying to recuperate. Stars were beginning to shine in the dusk, and the crackle of the campfire drew me forward. It was so good to be around people again I didn't care what they thought of me. I've been a loner all my life, but those days out in the wilderness taught me one thing. I need people after all. I could almost hear Grandmother's soft voice, saying I told you so. *Okay, you were right. Are you happy now?* And grinned, for the first time in what felt like forever.

Even though I knew they didn't like me very much. They were people. I wasn't going to die out in the wilderness alone. That was worth the price of admission all by itself.

* * *

Anna bounced around the campfire, in theory apparently helping Mrs. Byrne, who was cooking.

Byrne was still gone off illegally hunting, I guessed, because he wasn't around. Mrs. Byrne was vibrating around the campfire like an aspen leaf, and she wouldn't meet anyone's eyes.

Until Anna almost knocked over the peculiar frying pan on legs sitting over the coals. Then she gave Anna the eye, without a word, and Anna went and sat down with her hands in her lap.

Two of the younger men reclined against logs. The clean-shaven older one who'd come to tell me I was a tenderfoot after I'd upchucked the first meal I'd had in days was gone, too, and I assumed he was with the arrogant Byrne.

It was a scene out of *Gunsmoke*, right down to the clothes. I kept my mouth shut about it this time.

I couldn't explain it by hallucination anymore, or by any rational reason. What else was I supposed to do? The only other explanation I could come up with was they were crazy. Or I was. It was pointless to point the one out to them, and dangerous to make an issue of the other, especially since they thought I had lost most of my marbles already.

"Is there anything I can do to help?" I asked, carefully not aiming the question directly at Mrs. Byrne. I couldn't seem to open my mouth around her without putting my foot wrong somehow.

She answered me anyway. "No. Thank you." She bent down as if to lift the lid off the frying pan, then straightened again and stared out into the dusk. She looked as if she wanted to swear about something, but she didn't. The firelight caressed her face, and it softened her features into something I hadn't quite expected of her.

I didn't realize I'd been staring till one of the men cleared his throat. The other one chuckled.

"You better not do that when Byrne comes back."

Mrs. Byrne whirled, her skirts narrowly missing both fire and frying pan. "Do what?"

"Uh, spit into the fire like that. Fred was spitting in the fire again."

Fred gave the other man a dirty look. He responded with a shrug.

"Never mind about Mr. Byrne. If I catch you spitting into the fire while I'm cooking again, I'll have your hide."

"No, ma'am. I am sorry." This was from Fred, who, so far as I could tell, hadn't spit in the fire, not since I'd been there, anyway.

Mrs. Byrne turned back to her frying pan, and the other man winked at me.

"Supper's ready," Mrs. Byrne said, irritation in her voice. "Where in heaven are they?" She stepped back from the fire and stared into the shadows. "Hush, all of you."

We hushed. She listened. All I could hear was the crackle of the fire and the occasional gust of wind through the trees. Apparently it was all she could hear, too, because her expression hadn't changed when she turned back and gestured to the man who wasn't Fred.

"Lift that up for me, if you would, Mick."

Mick obligingly stood up, took the doubled-over cloth from her, and lifted the pan to a nearby stump.

"Bring your plates," Mrs. Byrne said. "No point in letting it get cold."

The stew smelled wonderful. My mouth watered, but I didn't step forward.

Mrs. Byrne looked up. "There's a spare plate or two over in that packsaddle."

I gave her a grateful smile and went to the pile of gear.

I opened the saddlebag, then stopped, staring. It was full of what I guess you'd call camping gear, if you were playing Old West. There was some strange-looking mechanical stuff, and some pieces of fabric, and dishes. The tin plates were like the ones Granddad liked to use when we went camping when I was a kid, and the enameled mugs were familiar for the same reason. I shrugged and grabbed what I needed, and went back to the fire.

Mrs. Byrne served my plate, but stopped about halfway.

"Hey," I said. "I'm hungry."

She chuckled. "Let's see if you can keep this down first, Mr. McManis."

I did a double-take. Nobody'd ever called me Mister before. "Most people call me Chuck."

Her smile vanished, and she bent back to her stewpot. "Go sit down, Mr. McManis, and eat your supper."

Oooookay. You put your foot in it again. Somehow. So I sat down.

She was right, and I knew it. It was hard to be smart about it, though. Thick gravy covering venison and potatoes and some kind of root vegetable I didn't recognize, and onions. I tried not to think about where the venison had come from because once we got back to civilization I was going to have to report them.

I was between bites, letting my stomach decide I wasn't trying to poison it, when I happened to look over at Mrs. Byrne, who was gazing out into the woods again.

I wanted to do something to say thank you, but somehow it didn't seem like a good idea.

I could compliment her cooking, though. "That's good stew." I stopped as she gave me a look that said, as plain as day, that I called her by her name at my own risk.

Then she smiled at me. "It is an awkward situation," she said. "We haven't been properly introduced, Mr. McManis. My name is Mrs. William Byrne."

I blinked. That was a bit formal. Now that I thought about it, I knew I'd heard that name before today. Byrne. Byrne. Couldn't place it, and it was going to bug me till I did.

She'd certainly put me at a distance, though. "Mrs. Byrne," that brought a gleam to her eye, and a look of approval to her face, "your stew and my stomach seem to have reached an agreement. May I have some more, please?"

"Give yourself a few minutes."

I sighed. The other men had called her ma'am when they weren't Mrs. Byrne-ing her. I could do that. "Yes, ma'am. I feel okay, though." Even though my stomach felt a bit queasy, I wanted more food. It wasn't as bad as earlier.

"I'm sure you do-" she stopped mid-sentence, then strode off into the dark, ladle in hand and skirts whipping around her legs. Anna started to follow, but Fred grabbed her. "You stay here, young lady."

She glared at him, but stayed.

We all waited. The moments stretched out, in a kind of odd, expectant dread.

"I told you I'd be back when I got back, woman." It was Byrne, sounding angry. "Don't you talk back to me."

I could hear Mrs. Byrne's voice, but I couldn't hear her words.

Byrne certainly could, though, and whatever she'd said had ticked him off.

"What do you mean, he's still here? Sponging off of us, wasting our food. I suppose he'll want to borrow a horse next."

They came in to the firelight. I stood. "If you're talking about me, sir, I'm sorry I imposed on you. If you'll point me towards the nearest telephone, I'll be on my way." Six sets of eyes stared at me as if I'd grown two heads. The silence grew as if it fed on the firelight, until I couldn't stand it any longer. "What?"

"Tele-phone?"

"Hush, Anna," Mrs. Byrne said without ever taking her eyes off me. "Mr. McManis, we're three days from the nearest telegraph, if that's what you mean."

"It doesn't matter what he means. Apologize to my wife, McManis."

Huh? "For what?"

"What do you think for?"

"It's all right, William."

"No, it damned well is not."

"I'm sorry, ma'am." I started to back out of the circle of firelight.

The whole thing had to be a hallucination, had to be had to be had to be. I kept backing up, managing not to fall over a log or anything else but I wasn't going to take my eyes off that band of lunatics until they vanished.

Please, I prayed to whatever gods there are out there, *please* let me wake up. I'll go back to Denver and do what Dad tells me and I'll never be stupid again.

I could still see the glow of the campfire through the trees. I kept going for a few hundred more yards, until I almost fell into a hot pool which brought me to my senses.

It's a nightmare, that's all. I sat down next to the warmth of the spring. Tomorrow I would wake up in my room at the Inn, or better yet in my own room back in Denver. It was all going to be okay when I woke up.

I lay for a long time staring into the darkness. Old Faithful went off three times, and I could hear the swoosh and splash of other geysers doing what geysers do. The pool I lay next to was quiescent, the occasional gas bubble churning up from the depths and breaking the surface with a watery belch. A couple of times I heard voices coming from the camp, but I ignored them.

I wished like anything I'd gotten that second helping of venison stew. The bit I'd eaten wasn't enough, and God knew when I'd get more.

The bugs all found me again, too. I guess I was the tastiest thing they could find.

There's got to be more people around. They can't all be nutcases. Someone will know where there's a phone. Someone will have a car.

* * *

I'm not sure I ever did sleep that night. It was about one in the morning when I realized I was going to have to go back to the Byrnes' camp. They might be crazy, but dying out in the wilderness was a pretty stupid alternative to swallowing my pride.

Not till the morning, though. I wasn't about to go charging into their camp in the middle of the night. I'd get myself shot. Byrne probably would be proud of himself.

Mrs. Byrne wouldn't. But Mrs. Byrne wasn't exactly pleased with me, either. Granted, I probably hadn't seen her husband at his best, but I couldn't see why she stayed with him. He was taking his role as pioneer manly man way too far, and why she'd agreed to play her part was beyond me.

I watched the moon set over the hill. It was just an uptilted sliver, which meant I'd been out here longer than I'd thought. I tried to count the days, but they all ran together. My brain wasn't working at full capacity, and hadn't been for what felt like forever.

If I hadn't been out wandering around in the middle of the night, if I hadn't insisted on following Granddad's will against Dad's wishes, if I hadn't been so stubborn about staying with Granddad and Grandmother all my life, if I hadn't...

* * *

I awoke to three faces looming over me. Anna was the first to speak.

"You're coming back with us." She sounded pretty authoritative, even when you considered her high-pitched voice. "You made Sister unhappy."

I blinked up at her.

"She worries about people."

I found my voice. "What about Mr. Byrne?"

"Don't worry about him," said Fred. "If he puts up a fuss, he's a bigger numskull than I thought he was."

"He did put up a fuss," Anna said, grinning. "Sister put up a bigger one."

"Look," I said, "I don't want to be the cause of an argument."

"Too late!" Anna did a little skip. "Get up."

Mick grabbed my arm and pulled. I scrambled to my feet, and realized they were all looking smug.

"Is there something I don't know?"

"Yeah," said Mick. "You changed everything, and we appreciate the-" He coughed, catching Fred's eye. "We appreciate it."

When we got back to the campsite, Byrne was nowhere to be seen, but Mrs. Byrne was dishing up bacon and biscuits with great good cheer. My stomach growled, but I remembered the day before and shuddered. She caught my eye and smiled. "Welcome back, Mr. McManis. There's oatmeal if the bacon doesn't suit you."

I couldn't face the bacon. "Oatmeal would be great."

She handed Anna her plate, and reached for the lid of a pot sitting at the edge of the coals. Taking the big spoon in her other hand, she stirred the contents before dishing them out into a bowl.

I didn't know oatmeal smelled good. Mrs. Byrne handed me the bowlful, and the container of honey they were using on the biscuits.

"You look like you could use some sweetening," was all she said.

There wasn't any butter, but it didn't matter. I and my stomach were both quite content to let the sweet stuff slide down my throat, washed down with coffee, also sweet.

Mrs. Byrne carried off a plate of bacon and biscuits, to the ticked-off Byrne, I assumed, and the rest of us relaxed.

Anna turned to me with the air of someone chosen to tell important news. "You're going to be staying with us till we go back to Fort Ellis. We just got here yesterday, and we don't want to turn around that quick."

"Okay." Then I thought about what she'd said, and shrugged. There wasn't much I could do about it. I still hadn't been able to reconcile what I saw before me with anything remotely approaching reality. All I knew was that I could feel the food in my stomach, see and hear the people around me.

When I got to civilization, and found a telephone, *then* I could find reality.

In the meantime, I had food, shelter, and people. Compared to what I'd possessed forty-eight hours ago, that was saying quite a lot.

"So, what's on the agenda for today?" I asked Anna.

"Lots. We're going to go watch geysers again."

"Again?"

"While you were sleeping yesterday we walked and walked and walked. Sister says you slept all day. She wouldn't go far from the camp. It made Mr. Byrne mad. He kept saying, I dragged you all the way here, woman." Anna giggled.

A few minutes later, Mrs. Byrne reappeared, with two empty plates. No one acted as if this was odd, and Mrs. Byrne started doing dishes, calling Anna to her for help. Anna went willingly, after a glance from her fellow conspirator Mick.

I picked up my oatmeal bowl and took it to where the women were working. "Can I help?" I asked. It seemed the least I could do.

Mrs. Byrne glanced up at me, startled. I looked around. The other men were gone. "Thank you. You could dry for me."

So I took the cloth she indicated and dried dishes. "I hope I haven't made things too hard for you."

Her eyes went back to her work. "One more mouth isn't that much work."

That hadn't been what I meant, but I wasn't about to put my foot into it again. "Maybe not, but it means a lot to me. I don't want to be in your way."

She grimaced, but Anna beat her to the punch. "You aren't, except for-"

"Anna. If you can't behave, you'll have to stay in camp today."

Anna's playfulness dissolved, leaving her more solemn than I'd thought her capable of. "Yes, ma'am."

Now go wash yourself up, and we'll have some fun."

Anna's smile reappeared. "Yes, ma'am," she replied, in an entirely different tone.

I couldn't resist. I snapped the towel at her. She squealed, and ran, and when I turned to look at Mrs. Byrne, her glance was approving.

"Mr. McManis, that was totally uncalled for," she said, in a mock-stern tone.

"Oh, I don't think so. We don't want her misbehaving, after all."

Mrs. Byrne's laughter stopped abruptly. I turned, already knowing what, or rather who, I would see.

I'm not sure which of us William Byrne was actually scowling at. Mrs. Byrne tugged on my dishtowel, and I let go.

"He was helping me, William."

"Where's Anna?"

"I sent her to get something for me. For heaven's sake."

Byrne's face softened a bit. He does care for her, I thought, even if he does have his head up his butt. That made it all the more hard to swallow his next statement, pronounced as if jerked from his mouth by brute force.

"Thank you, McManis. For helping my wife. But if you're going to be traveling with us, by God you're going to observe the proprieties. Both of you. Just because we're out in the middle of the wilderness doesn't excuse either of you."

Huh?

Mrs. Byrne sighed. "Yes, dear." She turned to me. "Go on."

I left the two of them, standing toe to toe, and walked away. I heard splashing and thought, why not? I could have slept, but Mrs. Byrne would have felt like she'd have to watch over me again, and I'd caused her enough trouble as it was.

* * *

I hadn't realized it, but we were camped a lot closer to one of the geysers than I, for one, was certainly comfortable with.

The splashing was Castle Geyser, looking pretty much the same as the last time I'd seen it, how long ago? I found a comfortable log to lean against and sat to watch, my eyelids drooping. *It should go off much higher than this.* Granddad's voice came back to me. "Castle," he'd said, "always makes you think it's not worth standing around waiting for, and then, as you're about to walk away, it lets off with something pretty special." I shifted my weight, brushed a pinecone or two out from under me, and waited, half dozing in the dappled shade.

Sure enough, after a while of here-a-splash, there-a-splash, a great gout of water shot up into the sky, letting out a bullroar that made me shudder in memory. But the ground never moved, the water never came close to me. *Dammit, I'm too tired to be scared.* Now wasn't then, this wasn't Grand, there was no earthquake, and I wasn't going to be wiped out like one of the mosquitoes I slapped, barely noticing them as I wiped my hands on my jeans. They were small potatoes, as Granddad used to say. Not even worth the complaining over.

Not that I still didn't miss my bug dope. I looked like I'd been buckshot, but right then I didn't care.

I sensed, rather than saw, another person standing nearby watching. When the water finally stopped splashing, I turned and shouted over the roar of the steam. "That was a good one."

"Yeah, it was," Fred shouted back. "Wanna come wait for Old Faithful with us?"

"Why not?"

I got back to my feet with some effort and we strolled back through the geyserite meadow, past pools and steam and rainbows. Without all the buildings and other scars from man, it looked surreal.

When I wake up from all this, I'm going to have to write it all down. No one's seen it like this since the first explorers. No one will ever see it like this again.

Lazy white clouds slid across the sky, moving shadows against the ground, cooling us as we walked, then gliding on and letting the August sun pound down again. I was past the stage of sunburn now, not that it mattered.

I could see the rest of the group at Old Faithful from some distance.

"What are they doing?" I asked Fred. "Looking to get scalded?"

"They're gonna try to stop it up. See what happens."

I stopped dead. "They're *what?*"

He shook his head. I could see he was chalking my shock up to my general insanity. I couldn't chalk this up to *their* general insanity, though.

This place was a national treasure. Didn't they *know* that? I began to run, my ankle complaining for the first time in a while. I ignored it.

By the time I got to them, I was out of breath. Before I could catch it enough to say anything, Byrne said, "McManis. We need another back. Come here."

I didn't move. I don't think I could have if God himself had ordered me to. Those idiots had a log the size of Mt. Rushmore poised to shove, big end first, into the opening of the geyser. They shoved. It didn't move. Stuck on something, I guessed. Good. Flaming *idiots.*

One of Great-Grandmother's stories flashed through my mind. "It exploded everywhere. I had my little sister back at a safe distance with me, although it was all I could do to keep her from running up and getting herself hurt, but the men were dodging branches, and rocks, and that big log they dropped down the hole came shooting out like someone had pitched a javelin. I've never seen anything like it."

"Dammit, McManis, get over here." Byrne broke my stunned recollection.

I opened my mouth. Nothing came out. I closed it, swallowed, and tried again. "Not on your life. What are you trying to do? Kill yourselves? Not to mention the damage you're doing to the geyser."

Well, I'd gotten my point across, as Byrne's purple face proved, but I was beyond tactful. I stepped forward, ready to shove that log back where it came from, when my foot slipped, and I almost landed flat on my butt on the geyserite. That stuff is like walking on a skating rink, especially when it's wet. God, I missed the boardwalks. And the rangers. What I needed right now was an army of them.

As I sat there watching in horrified disbelief, Byrne and Mick shoved on the log again, and it slipped almost in slow motion down the hole. It was a loose fit. I swear I felt the rattle in the ground as it slid.

I groaned.

At first things were pretty anticlimactic. Nothing happened. We all stood there, everybody else in excited anticipation, me in frozen horror. I heard Anna over on the other side of the crater, whining at Mrs. Byrne, who, exactly as my great-grandmother had told me she'd done with *her* sister, had a firm grip on her arm. "Let me go, Sister, I can't see."

"You can see perfectly well."

"It's not going to go off."

I walked carefully around the mound and over to them.

"It's going to go off, Anna."

She tried to jerk her arm away, but Mrs. Byrne hung on. "I want to watch! Besides, you're hurting me."

I shook my head, and said, "It's dangerous. Mrs. Byrne's smart."

Just then, we heard a shout from the mound. "She's getting ready to blow!"

Anna jerked again. I reached around and grabbed her other arm. Mrs. Byrne gave me a grateful look. Anna glared at me. We all turned to watch the spectacle.

The ground rumbled. I heard another shout from the men. "We did it! We stopped up the geyser!"

I yelled, "And aren't you proud of yourselves for ruining a national treasure."

They turned and stared at me. As if they'd never thought about the consequences. Well, damn, I thought, even if there wasn't anyone here who could stop them didn't mean they had the right to be this stupid.

If they'd permanently ruined it...

But I knew they hadn't. Somehow. As it was, a malicious sort of glee overtook me. If the same thing happened to them as had to the people Great-Grandmother'd been with... I turned to look at Mrs. Byrne, who was watching me with a combination of curiosity and worry. "I have Anna, Mr. McManis, if you want to go."

Her words were interrupted by a mighty roar. The ground shook like we were at the center of an earthquake. I went flat on the ground, praying the events of a few days ago weren't about to repeat themselves.

The men froze. Anna, I noticed out of the one non-terrified corner of my mind, was no longer fighting her sister's grip. They crouched. I stayed down.

Then it happened. Old Faithful was going to be damned before it wasn't faithful. First came the log, shooting up out of the crater like it had been pitched by a giant in a caber-tossing contest, arching up into the air before it came crashing down onto the geyserite, narrowly missing Byrne, who broke into a run. They all ran, slipping and sliding in the muddy water as the geyser spewed rocks and tree limbs and everything else they'd shoved down the hole. Somebody's shirt went sailing through the air like a flag of surrender before it landed on Mick's head. He went down with a thud, scraping the still-steaming cloth off of his head with a howl of pain.

The ground slowly stopped shaking. The geyser eventually ran out of rocks to fling and contented itself with the longest display of fountaining water I'd ever seen it throw. I sat up and leaned weakly on the log I'd gone behind. Mrs. Byrne straightened. Anna escaped her at last, and ran to the men who, now safely across the Firehole River, bent and wheezed and swore, their occasional shouted word making it to us over the splashing.

I couldn't help myself. The guffaw burst out of me like, well, like Old Faithful itself.

Mrs. Byrne stared at me.

"Mr. McManis?" she said, backing up a step or two.

I leaned over the tree trunk and laughed till I cried. I couldn't catch my breath. It wasn't just the spectacle I'd witnessed. I felt like I'd been pole-axed. I stared at Mrs. Byrne, who stared back at me. I opened my mouth, closed it again. Mrs. Byrne backed up another step.

It had all happened. Exactly as Great-Grandmother had described it to me, the rapt five-year-old sitting on the rug in front of her easy chair in her room at the nursing home, less than a month before she died. I remembered it as well as if it had happened yesterday.

And here she was, in front of me, backing slowly away with fear in her eyes, a younger version of herself. Brown eyes, no longer clouded and greyish as they'd been when I'd known her, but sharp and as rich as melted caramel. Her hair was thicker, and brown instead of white, but the wave over her forehead was the same. As I watched, she reached up and brushed it back. The hand that performed the little motion was young and strong, not veined and arthritic, but it was the same gesture.

My brain shut down. I don't know how else to describe it. Everything around me became fuzzy but for her. The ground rumbled beneath my feet.

"Mr. McManis?"

I heard her voice as if from a far distance. Pools of black swarmed into my vision. And I don't remember what happened after that.

Hallucination? Or what?

Repeating History is available at all major retailers.

BOOKS BY M.M. JUSTUS

Much Ado in Montana

Cross-Country: Adventures Alone Across America and Back

TALES OF THE UNEARTHLY NORTHWEST

Sojourn

TIME IN YELLOWSTONE

Repeating History
True Gold
"Homesick"
Finding Home

Carbon
River
Press

ABOUT THE AUTHOR

M.M. Justus's first visit to Yellowstone National Park was at age four, where it snowed on the Fourth of July. She spent most of her childhood summers in the back seat of a car, traveling with her parents to almost every national park west of the Mississippi and a great many places in between.

She holds degrees in British and American literature and history and library science, and a certificate in museum studies. In her other life, she's held jobs as far flung as hog farm bookkeeper, music school secretary, professional dilettante (aka reference librarian), and museum curator, all of which are fair fodder for her fiction.

Her other interests include quilting, gardening, meteorology, and the travel bug she inherited from her father, including multiple trips back to her favorite Grand Geyser and the rest of Yellowstone. She lives on the rainy side of the Cascade mountains in Washington state within easy reach of her other favorite national park, Mt. Rainier.

Please visit her website and blog at http://mmjustus.com, on Facebook at https://www.facebook.com/M.M.Justusauthor, on Twitter @mmjustus, or on Pinterest at http://www.pinterest.com/justus1240/.

Made in the USA
Columbia, SC
15 November 2017